THE END OF THE GAME

THE END OF THE GAME

MICHAEL FIDDIAN

First published in 2022 by Popcorn Press, an imprint of Fair Play Publishing
PO Box 4101, Balgowlah Heights, NSW 2093, Australia

www.popcornpress.com.au

ISBN: 978-1-925914-39-9
ISBN: 978-1-925914-40-5 (ePub)

Cover design and typesetting by Lisa Rafferty
Printed in Sydney by SOS Print

All inquiries should be made to the Publisher via sales@fairplaypublishing.com.au

A catalogue record of this book is available from the National Library of Australia.

Contents

PREFACE

There is a reason this book is set in September 1992—it is a year after Chris Lewis was racially abused in a Grand Final, three months after the Mabo Decision and two months before Prime Minister Paul Keating's Redfern Park speech. Nicky Winmar's famous stance at Victoria Park came a year later.

It is two years before Damian Monkhorst and Michael Long weren't allowed to speak at a media conference about racism and the AFL introduced their Racial Vilification Policy—a time when what was said on the field apparently stayed on the field, but attitudes towards race and Aboriginal players were supposedly beginning to shift.

If only times had really changed.

CHAPTER 01

SATURDAY

It had to hurt—not just a bit, not just for a second, but really hurt, and for a long time. The captain, Mitch, had already done his bit, and made the rest of the boys wince. Then Basher, the big, quick—but intellectually challenged—half back flanker had raised the bar to a level no-one had thought possible.

Now it was Tom's turn.

He looked around the group who surrounded him and met their gazes evenly. Six months ago he could never have imagined what he was about to do or that he would be in the place where he was about to do it. A whitewashed rectangular room with opaque glass and a smell that could only exist in this kind of environment—one of sweat, Dencorub and dank humanity; it seemed the perfect place for him to have to complete the feat which now lay before him.

It wasn't like he was scared, or worried—he knew pain in different ways and also knew that this pain would go away as soon as the task ended; it was more that he wanted to get a good reaction. His last three weeks had been pitiful, and given where they were in the year, he thought it was time to make a statement.

"Okay, boys," he declared. "Prepare to squirt."

He put the nail from his thumb and forefinger underneath the strapping tape, and slowly, as slowly as he possibly could, he began to lift it. Instead of ripping it quickly as if it was one big Band-Aid, he did it deliberately, making every effort to shred every follicle of hair on his calf and ankle. He didn't have much to show—he was never particularly hairy anyway, and doing this task every week meant that his ankle and lower calf were as smooth as glass—but he still gave it his best shot. It took him ten seconds to get the first piece off—it hurt, but he dared not show it, and he dragged out the amount of time it took to take each strip off. To cries of "Aww, come on!", "Enough already!" and "This is torture, and it's not even my leg!", he removed the seven pieces of tape on his left leg.

As the last one came off, he saw a trickle of blood appear just below the ball of his ankle and roll onto his heel and then the concrete floor. He cried out with triumph, "Watch out, gents, she's a bleeder!"

The boys didn't know he'd cut himself on the frame of his bike two nights before and all he had done was lift off a fresh scab, so he was able to make a huge deal of his achievement. One of the team, Whitey, went a shade of grey no-one had seen before and forced his way through the team towards the single toilet in the rooms. When the team heard his vomit splash at the bottom of the yellowing bowl they cheered; Tom knew he would be crowned today's champion. Later on he was described by the coach as "Bleeding impressive", and the boys had laughed raucously, knowing the compliment had nothing to do with Tom's footballing ability.

There was a feeling in the change room that was different than what was normal after a win; the thrill of a victory being replaced by an expectant feeling of excitement. The team had just won through to the regional Grand Final, something that had not occurred in their age group for twenty-two years. It was an even bigger deal because no Duneldin team had made any Grand Final in more than a decade.

Amongst the team there was no real surprise—they had been the best side in the competition and they knew it, but to actually make it provided a feeling of relief. The game they had just won was tighter than they had expected too—in front by 22 points at half time, and where they would normally have expected to run away with it in the second half, they only got home by 14 in the end. The players had celebrated on the ground, and come into the rooms congratulating each other—and then gone through the ritual torture of removing the strapping tape—but they had not been happy with what had happened on the field, knowing that they should have won by at least 15 goals. The feeling as soon as they were off the ground was one of relief, not exhilaration, but now this was changing as they started to imagine what the week and the following Saturday would hold.

Fitz, the coach of the team, had not laid it on too thick but had made it clear what his expectations were.

"Now, lads, (every one of his speeches started this way, and there was a prize amongst the team for those who could impersonate it the best at inappropriate times), we got over the line, but only just. We're better than what we showed today, and we've got a week to fix it. That's what training's for." He paused, and scanned the small room where the boys had gathered to make sure every eye met his. Unwaveringly, they did.

"Now for most of you, this week will be a brand-new experience. Hmph! It's almost a brand-new experience for the whole town. Seventeen years since the town's been in a Granny! You can all expect the place to go a bit nuts. That's all right, it's only to be expected.

"Be ready for it—you won't hear about much else this week—school, the paper, your mates, maybe even your families will be peppering you with advice and information. Most important thing is to remember that the time for us to go berserk is after the siren next weekend. Until then, as far as I'm concerned, it's business as usual. We train the same, we prepare the same, we think the same way about the game. The rest is noise, and we have to work out a way to ignore that noise if we're gonna do what we set out to. We set ourselves in February for this, and it's within our grasp." He paused.

Tom started playing footy cliché bingo in his head, and was close to completing a whole row. He aimlessly wondered if there was a book of obvious and well-worn phrases that was sent to coaches at the start of each year and they just made their way through it line by line, then brought his mind back to the coach.

"Don't forget to enjoy it though, it's a once-in-a-lifetime opportunity! Bloody bloody!"

The boys smiled at another one of their coach's verbal tics. Fitz breathed in deeply, trying to calm himself, but his eyes dazzled and a wide, engaging smile appeared on his thin face. "I'm proud of all of ya, but let's get on with the business. Now hit the showers, pack, and go home and get a good night's sleep—I don't want to hear about anyone goin' out partyin' and walkin' the streets at 3 a.m. lookin' for trouble."

Michael Bennett, the half forward who had kicked an important settling goal in the last quarter, mimicked, "We won't be bloody lookin' for trouble, we'll be bloody lookin' for you!", and with that the boys all roared. Fitz tried to resume his speech, but he knew the boys had bested him, so he laughed, and raised his hands.

"That you might, that you might. All right. Well done and well played. See you on Tuesday."

The boys stood up, and the tension was released. They climbed down from the tiered benches of the room and headed out to the larger change room, where the crowd had been waiting for them to finish their meeting. Normally they would be expected to clear out quickly, but because they were the only one of the town's three teams to make the finals, there was no real rush, and there was a feeling that they should savour this moment, knowing it was an occasion that demanded appreciation. Some boys headed for the showers, while others examined themselves for the expected cuts and bruises a game always brought them. The five Indigenous boys in the team stood in their normal corner, laughing at each other and still playing with a football, kicking it from one to the other as if it was a hacky sack. Tom looked at them and wondered if they were thinking about heading back out and playing another game. Every time they came off the field they looked fresh and without a care, while he was exhausted and only wanted to leave the sheds and wander either home or to a waiting car so he could go and lie in the bath for a few hours.

It seemed the number of parents and friends who were in the rooms after the games had multiplied, and everywhere Tom looked there were adults, teenagers and young kids walking around, patting the boys on the back and congratulating them. Despite his initial surprise, Tom willingly accepted their praise. He had played his role well, stopping his opponent from having any real influence, and getting a few important possessions, but he knew that the real accolades belonged to some of the other players, and he hoped they were getting them.

After about three quarters of an hour of talking about the game, reliving the key moments and wondering about next week, Tom noticed most of the boys had packed their gear into their club-provided footy bags, and were making their way towards the exit. Tom was happy to join them. He made a point of saying thank you and goodbye to Fitz—who paused, looked him in the eye and told him he was good, better than good, which made Tom blush—and then he walked out into the fading sunshine of a clear winter's afternoon.

The coach's post-game address and the added amount of people in the rooms post match had crystallised something for Tom—that the next week would be something that would take on a life of its own, and that the idea of keeping a lid on it would be almost impossible. He had felt the joy of the crowd at the end of the game and noticed that more people had spilled onto the ground and wanted to pat them on the back than ever before—even though they hadn't played well. In the rooms he had his back slapped by people he had never seen before, let alone spoken to, and people he had only passed in the street tousled his hair and commended him on some of the play he had been involved in, even mistaking him for other players who had taken part in what was being described. There had been times in the change room where the buzz and anticipation were so tangible that his mind was spinning, and he knew that not much would change in the next seven days.

It had not taken long for Tom to realise the influence that Aussie Rules had on the town that he and his mother had moved to. Tom had been in the town less than a day before it was obvious he was being sized up by the locals as to what position he would play.

In one of the first conversations he had ever had with a resident, he was asked what team he followed, what position he played and even what his favourite brand of boots were. Two minutes later he had been asked by someone else—who seemed to be a replica of the person he had just spoken to—who his favourite player of all time was and if he believed in fate when it came to Collingwood Grand Final sides of the 1970s. Tom had not known how to answer either time; he soon realised he was seen as being weird for not having an immediate response, in contrast to what he saw as being weird by being asked such random questions in mid-January in the middle of summer. He would be asked these kinds of questions throughout the next few weeks, and even by then he had wondered what life would be like here in the middle of winter.

On the night of their arrival, Tom and his mum Jenny had gone out for dinner. They had chosen the pub that seemed the grandest. There were three to choose from and only one looked like it had actual people in it, and immediately he had been struck by the fact that the walls of the bistro were lined with photographs of the town's team, the Bombers. Tom's gaze was drawn to the rows of old sepia-toned photographs that lined where he was sitting. They were shots of old football teams—photos of men who looked aggressively at the camera, lined up on individual chairs or benches, with the smallest one always down the front nestling an old and weather-beaten football.

Tom smiled—he had seen plenty of these types of photos; indeed, he had been in them, and he knew about the bravado that went with the sessions. Boys would try to see who could push their biceps out to make them look bigger, trying to make themselves believe that they were about to go into a glorious battle. Most likely the photos were taken at the beginning of the season before anyone on the team knew how good or bad they were going to be, and they were as much about recording optimism as they were about recording history. Tom's gaze moved across the photos—the ones nearest him were dated 1957 through to 1974 but as he tracked backwards they went back as far as the 1930s.

As he looked carefully, he noticed the threads of commitment running through them—the same players in the photos, sometimes in sitting positions, sometimes standing, but nonetheless, there were men who seemed to have lived the entirety of their lives before his eyes. One man, Jim Thomas, was always in the same place in the photos with the same look on his face—one of a knowing determination, one eyebrow raised as if he knew something the photographer didn't. Tom wondered how the teams had gone in the years Jim Thomas played for them—did he have that look because they continually lost, or because he wanted them to keep winning? He also noticed that in one year—1968—Thomas' hair had grown much longer than any of the previous years, but by 1969 it was back to normal. It made Tom wonder what had happened to him in that year, and what had made him break out of the monotony of the previous six years' haircuts. He moved so close to the photos, so desperately trying to get an understanding of the town from them, that his breath started to fog on the glass, until he realised he was so close that his own reflection was looking at him. He saw his sandy hair, wide green eyes and flat nose, and as he did he stood back, seeing a history of a town in sepia, and he wondered if there would ever be a time when people would be leaning in, examining a photo of him.

A couple of days after their arrival they were sitting in their kitchen, looking at the unopened boxes, piles of paper and bubble wrap that neither wanted to deal with, when they heard a knock at the door. Jenny raised an eyebrow, and looked at Tom. "Were you expecting someone?"

Tom laughed. "Of course, Mum. All my new friends are here to play with my toys." Jenny hopped off the kitchen stool and walked to the door. Tom heard her open it, and then a huge voice fill the entrance. "Jenny? Frank Collins. Nice to meet you. Welcome to Duneldin."

"Thanks. Nice to meet you too." There was a pause, and Tom winced at the awkward silence. He heard his mother plug it. "What brings you here, Frank? Are you a neighbour coming to say hi?"

"Not exactly. I mean it's a small town so we're all neighbours, but it's not that. Actually, I'm the president of Duneldin Football Club. Given you're new at the paper and you'll be writing about us, we're probably going to be working together a bit, and I was in the neighbourhood. I thought I'd drop in and introduce myself."

"Oh! Right. Thanks. Come on in then."

Frank walked in, and dominated the room as soon as he entered it. He saw Tom, and his eyes lit up. "Hello! Who are you?"

"Hey. I'm Tom."

"Play footy?"

"Yep."

"What position?"

"Wherever they want me, usually. Mostly in the backline."

"How old are you?"

"Sixteen. Seventeen in August."

"Great. We're a couple short in the 18s. See you down at the club in a few weeks for rego. Know where the club is?"

"Sort of. Over that way." Tom's arm flailed non-descriptively.

"Haven't been there for a feed yet? You have to. It's the best."

Jenny walked into the room, and laughed at Tom and Frank. "So you've met Tom then. What has he told you?"

"That he can play footy."

"Well, of course he can. He's been obsessed with it since he was little. I've been trying to convince him that the best way to get to know the town is to start playing."

"Well, you'd be right. Particularly here. Has he been playing long?"

"Ever since he was given a toy Kangaroo with a blue and white jumper on it when he was born."

"Really? The Kangaroos?"

"Yep." Tom didn't want to sound defensive, but couldn't help it.

"You've had a few lean old years. Never thought of changing teams?"

"Are you serious? You can do that?"

"No, not really. Who's your favourite player?"

"Use to be the Krakouers, but now it's Wayne Schwass." Frank raised an eyebrow, which Tom didn't understand. "Okay. Why the Krakouers?"

"'Cos they used to talk to each other without speaking. You ever seen anyone else do that?"

Frank paused, and looked at Tom and then Jenny. "No, actually I haven't. Never heard it put like that either. Are you too smart to be a footy player?"

"I'm too smart not to be."

"Ha!"

Jenny looked at Frank. "What can we do for you, Frank? I'm sure you weren't just walking past with a housewarming present."

Tom soon realised that this visit was about as random as the rising of the sun—Frank had dropped in to talk about how the club and the local paper, that Jenny now ran, might be able to help each other out. Jenny had admired out loud that the club would ever need helping out, but Frank, in his wisdom, had suggested that partnerships were long things and that you never knew when they might be needed to be called on. In an off-the-cuff, almost nonchalant way, Jenny noted that the club probably had better carpet and fittings in its social rooms than her office, and Frank laughed uproariously. "Of course we do! The carpet company, the plumbers, the carpenters—they all sponsor the club!"

Jenny, for all her city sharpness, still failed to make the connection. "So, they pay you in taps and new shag pile? How does anyone make any money doing that?"

"Easy! Where do you think all of the players and their families go to get their kitchens refitted and carpets redone? It's a requirement of playing for the club that you support the sponsors. Tom will be expected to do it too, if he gets a game. Money's a wheel in small towns, Jenny—you make it, then spend it in a shop, then they come back to yours and spend what you gave them." He paused, and lifted up the sleeve of his business shirt and noticed the time. "Look, I've got to get back to the office, but are you two busy? There are a couple of things worth mentioning about the club, but it's easier to show them to you. Might make it easier to understand."

Jenny raised an eyebrow at Tom, then smiled. "Nah, we're not busy. Just more boxes to unpack and fights to have about furniture placement. It would do us good to go for a walk."

They left the house, and Frank strode purposefully down the street, each footstep hitting the pavement as though he was angry with the concrete. Tom figured they would walk straight to the clubrooms and he would show them around, but instead he took them to the centre of town.

Duneldin only had one strip of shops, but it was long, running about 500 metres. There was a service station at each end, and what seemed to Tom like the basic necessities needed to keep a town alive. Supermarket, bakery, butcher, lone bank, hardware store, real estate agent. Some of the shops were empty, with a 'for lease' sign, while others were vibrant, with stands outside on the street and chairs and tables for the three different cafes. There were people happily wandering up and down, talking to each other—Tom could see what Frank meant about the money being spent within the community, and it going around in circles. Frank randomly pointed at shops, and gave a running commentary. "That butcher sponsors us, so does that real estate agent and that bakery."

Jenny looked at Frank. "But why? They're the only ones in town. They don't need to advertise."

"No, but they want everyone to see they're tied to the club. They don't give us much, but still, it's their signs they want up along the fence. Come on, I didn't want to you to see just this— there's somewhere that sums up our place in the town."

They kept walking, past the Chinese takeaway and fish and chip shop and then to a suburban street about 400 metres from where the shopping strip ended. Frank stopped suddenly, and Tom and Jenny both had to jump to stop from crashing into him. Frank turned to face the house that was across the street on the corner, a large brick-and-tile place with room for two cars in the garage and a wide expanse for a front lawn. He stood back and put his hands on his hips, then waved an arm at it. For a moment he didn't speak, and Jenny felt the need to break the silence. "Frank, this has been a great excursion, but what are we doing here? This is just a house."

"That's where you're wrong, Jen." Tom knew his mother hated being called Jen, but she let it slide. "This is the club's house. This shows you why we're so important in the town."

This time Tom took the bait. "But why? It's just a house on a street that looks like every other one in the town."

"Maybe. But let me tell you a story about this house. Six years ago, a man called Andrew Faulkner left the block that house is on to the club in his will. He didn't have a family, but he spent every Saturday night in our bistro, and he sold pies in the canteen for as long as he could stand up, so I guess he saw us as his clan. Anyway, when he left it, the board kicked around a few ideas about what to do with it until some genius—"

"Was it you?"

Frank smiled and nodded. "Some genius decided to run a fundraiser where past and present players at the club could help out build that house. Carpenters, plumbers, sparkies, they all gave their weekends and time after work to get it built pretty much for free, and then we sold it at a bit above market value as soon as it was finished. We relaid the turf, renovated the function rooms and the change rooms with the money, then still had enough left over to put some in the bank at the end. The whole club built it, and the whole club reaped the rewards."

"Wow." Jenny was genuinely impressed.

"Yep. That's what the team means to the town. No-one's going to be doing that for the town hall or the council chambers now, are they?"

"S'pose not."

"S'pose not. We give a lot to this town, and they give a lot back, regardless of whether we're winning or losing." Frank looked at his watch again. "Now I've really got to go. Do you know how to get home?"

"Yes, thanks."

"No worries. I'll be sure to be chatting with you soon, Jen, and Tom, this could be a big year for our 18s. Hope you're part of it. See you later." And with that he charged off down the street, leaving them in his wake. They looked at each other, bemused but enlightened, understanding more than they thought they would have at the end of his visit.

The time came for Tom to leave the change rooms. Normally he couldn't wait to get home, have a real shower—not one with cold water and the other boys all trying to wash mud off and protect their dignity at the same time—and eat his favourite post-match dinner of chicken fillets, sauce and chips. But the lure of the townspeople still out and around the grandstand talking about the next week held him back. He lingered, dropping in and out of conversations that both looked back at the game and looked forward to the next week. He finally got away from the stairs of the grandstand, with its new coat of paint but worn-down concrete steps, and was walking to the gates when a voice came at him out of the darkness.

"Hey, brudda, what's up?"

He was shocked by the sound, but smiled when he saw its origin. The voice came closer.

"Sorry, mate, did I shock you? I'll try and sound a bit more like a white fella, shall I? Well met, young man, and well played today."

Albert Edwards walked towards Tom, his dark skin glistening in the fading light. He was tall, but not in a way that made him stand out, and his slight frame hid a powerful core and strong arms—he could take and hand out big tackles, and his legs were long enough to allow him to look graceful when going at top speed. His hair was a mop that he never attended to, but he somehow managed to control it so that it never got in his way when he was playing. Tom knew he would have been purposefully waiting like that, using his brains and heritage to his advantage, a combination that had dropped him in trouble with more than a few people in his community. He was well known for the sharpness of his wit and the intelligence that existed behind his intense eyes, but more than anything, he was revered for his ability when it came to playing football. Players in his team knew how good he was, as did the rest of the competition. Even Fitz, who tried to treat everyone equally, regularly told them, "Just kick it to Albert", who was free to place himself wherever he wished on the field, without really worrying about what position he was supposed to line up in.

Tom told his mother Albert was a time machine—he had a way of slowing down the play when he got the ball, and he always seemed to have even half a second longer than anyone else to make a decision when he was threatened or when the game was in the balance. It was no surprise that today when the game had tightened, and it looked like Gracemere would run over them, that Albert forced himself into the game and almost through his own sense of will marched the team over the line. Tom marvelled at his skill but was often put off by his personality, and had never really been able to work out exactly where their friendship sat, despite how often they spent time together.

"Thanks. I think. I didn't do much."

"Maybe not, but you did what you needed to and then a bit more. I noticed the shepherds in the last quarter, even if Fitz didn't."

"Really?" No-one in the rooms had mentioned them, even

though Tom had been proud of his efforts, and one had given him a hard knock to the arm. "They weren't really shepherds—I think I fell into the guys more than actually shepherding."

"Doesn't matter. As he says," and they spoke in unison, trying their best to get the right sense of urgency and twang, "You beat your opposishun, your mate beats the opposishun, the team beats the opposishun!" There was euphoria in the way the sentence turned up at the end that made both of them smile.

"What's this week going to be like, for real?" Tom had been bursting to ask someone.

"Dunno. Big, I guess. I wasn't born the last time any team in this town made a Grand Final, neither was anyone in the team. I get the feeling we're going to be loved long time in the lead-up, and if we win we'll be heroes, but if we lose ..." He acted out a noose being strung up.

"Right. Shit. Kind of makes you wish you didn't make it."

"Mate, it's why we play. I can't wait for next week. It's going to be amazing, and when we win—"

"How can you be so sure?"

"Because our best will be better than their best."

Tom paused. "Wow. That's true. What a great way to put it."

"Can't claim it. It was Barassi talking about the 1970 Carlton team."

Before he had a chance to respond, Tom noticed a football rolling towards them, rolling on its point as if it had been perfectly dispatched. He moved towards it, but before he had the chance to grab it, Albert had stepped in front of him, and using the flat part on the top of his left foot, flipped the ball into the air. It arced serenely; he bounced it off his forehead, and then delivered the ball back perfectly to the two boys who had been kicking it on the oval, without ever touching it with his hands. Everyone—Tom, the boys, those who were playing and those still lingering, having a kick in the twilight—was amazed at the skill involved in the display. Tom found himself gawping at Albert with his mouth open. When Albert turned to look at him, he shrugged his shoulders and started laughing, an action that changed the internal lighting of his whole face. "Loosen up, mate. That's nothing compared to the crap I try at home—three broken windows and lots of time banished to my room this season will show you that."

The two young boys who had been kicking the ball nervously came over to Albert. They were about eleven and nine years old, and had on the training tops that the club gave the younger players at the start of every season. The shirts were grimy, and the kids themselves gave the sense of being unwashed and on the edge of decency. "Um, Edwards, can you come and have a kick with us for a while? We wanna get good and you know, well, can you come out?"

Albert looked at the boys, then lifted his head, and saw across the oval a group of four-wheel drives and Utes, surrounded by adults still in deck chairs, eskies open and picnic blankets out. He took a step back, then turned and frowned at Tom. He quickly shook his head no, and Tom laughed. "What's the matter?" Tom said. "Scared they'll show you up?"

"Nah, it's not that, it's just that …" His voice trailed off, but his eyes stayed glued across the ground, where the picnickers had started to pack up.

"What?" Tom was amazed at Albert's reluctance. Albert, who would kick a footy with anyone at any time as a way of feeling the leather in his hands. "Go on, they'll love it."

"They might love it, but their parents will … their parents

are just …"

Tom had no idea what Albert was referring to and blundered on. "Oh, they're just kids. Their parents won't care, they won't even notice. They've been on the beers all afternoon."

"That's the point." He looked at the vehicles again and sighed. "Goddamnit. Hey, what have I got to lose?" He turned back to the two children, who had their faces raised expectantly.

"Oh, come on, lads. Really? Really truly? Kick with you two?" He drooped his shoulders and put his head in his hands. Albert was clowning with the boys—both now knew he was going to give in, but doing things in a straightforward way wasn't the way Albert liked to deal with kids. Tom knew he had two younger brothers—probably about the same age as the two now in front of them—and this game must have been played out at the Edwards' house every night. "I'm knackered. Did you see me playing out there? Those big dudes wouldn't leave me alone."

"We know. We watched from over there." They vaguely pointed to the cars still parked. "You're our favourite player. You're everybody's favourite player. Even my mum thinks you're good at footy, and she has a go at everyone."

Albert laughed. "Oh, that's great. Tell your mum thanks. Which one is she then?"

"Mrs Thorpe."

"Thorpey! She's the loudest of the lot of them over there. Always got something to say, and every once in a while it's worth listening to. So she likes me, hey?"

"Sort of. She says she shouldn't, but she does." Albert raised his eyebrows, and a knowing smirk appeared on the corner of his mouth. The smaller one had removed himself from behind his brother and was now looking at Albert with wonder.

"What else does she say?"

"She says she wishes they'd let her pull the boots on because she'd be better than the fucking lot of you."

Both Tom and Albert laughed—at first they tried to stifle it but it became too hard to hide. Both of the boys had no idea why what they had said was funny, and they pressed on with their quest. "So, will you show us how to kick properly?"

"Oh, all right." He put his hands on his hips in fake exasperation, then paused, and jerked his thumb over his shoulder towards Tom. "What does your mum say about him?"

The eldest one seemed to notice Tom for the first time. "You? What number are you?"

Tom said, "31."

He paused, and then a look of recognition appeared in his eyes. "31? She says you're shit, but not as shit as some of the others."

Again, both older boys laughed out loud.

"Well, I'd say she's spot on." Albert had moved closer to the fence that separated the oval from the asphalt they had been standing on, and he walked to the gate, stepping onto the grass.

He started a clinic that Tom found hard to take in. Before he knew it, he was watching both boys improve their kicking, and Albert eventually had them running the same kind of handball drills that he did at training.

The older boy said, "I'm Peter. He's Darren."

Albert replied. "Nice to meet you, boys. You'll be good one day."

"Can you show us how to kick those goals?"

"Goals? Which ones?"

"You know, like the ones you kicked today." The boys ghosted kicking a ball over his shoulder, followed by the replication of the unique signalling of a goal umpire.

"I'll try, but half the time I don't know myself. They just kind of happen."

Tom knew Albert was lying, but he didn't let on. After every training session he saw Albert out by himself trying the most ridiculous attempts at goal from impossible angles—he had once seen him trying to kick a goal from the back of a slow-moving Ute that was outside of the fence, and only the ball scraping the inside of the post had stopped it from being preposterous.

The boys started taking potshots. Tom was still watching from outside the boundary, but knew it would be his job to fetch the ball and kick it back, and so started walking behind the goals, kicking the ball back to wherever Albert had moved to. The trio started from an easy spot, with Albert telling the boys they should look at the target to the last second and then look at the ball drop, and always kick drop punts. They then moved to sharper angles, where the two youngsters missed either side or often didn't make the distance at all, but not Albert. Every shot he took curled the right way at the right time, and went through. Tom was astonished— it was like the ball was expressively obeying the commands that Albert's foot was giving it, and Albert knew the level of control he had. The boys had picked up on this too—instead of taking turns, they handed the ball back to Albert when he tried to give it to them, and then pointed to where they wanted him to kick it from, a look of worship shared on their faces.

Fifteen minutes after the session had started, the conversation by the four-wheel drives had quietened, and there were nudges between the adults there to watch what was going on. A silence descended on the group, and when Tom looked at them he noticed the change in body language—they had gone from being relaxed, holding their stubbies and cans in a way that suggested there wasn't a care in the world. Now there was a tension in the way they stood, their hands by their sides, arms bent slightly—as if they were tensing for an attack that seemed the most unlikely thing in the artificial lights that had been turned on as the last of the crowd left for the day.

Like a scimitar, a voice cut through the quiet. "Peter! Darren! What do you think you're doin'!"

The two boys stood still, drawn towards the woman's screech.

"Nothing, Mum. Just playing footy with Albert," Peter replied, but there was foreboding in his voice.

"I can see that. Do you think I'm frickin' blind? What have I told you?"

"About what, Mum?"

"About … about who you choose to play with." There was an emphasis on the way she spat the words out that hung in the air long after the sentence finished.

"What-what—"

"Don't what me. I've told you to stay away from kids like that!"

Darren, the younger boy who had hardly said a word the whole time he was with Albert, spoke, surprising everyone. "What's wrong with him?"

Albert had walked across the oval towards the group who were now huddled behind the woman. "Good question, Mrs Thorpe. What's wrong with him?" He threw his shoulders back and eyeballed her defiantly.

"Stay out of this, Albert. It's got nothin' to do with you."

"Really? Of course it does. I'm pretty sure I'm the him you were talking about."

"Still got nothin' to do with you, smart mouth. Stay out of it." She looked down her nose at him, as if he was only just worth speaking to.

"Why? I'm right here." Albert's stance had changed, and it seemed as if he was bracing for a tackle. "You don't want your boys to play with me, even when they were the ones who came over and asked. Why not?"

Mrs Thorpe paused, and looked at the group behind her, her face returning to Albert with a look of disgust across it. She hissed, "I just … I want them to be careful who they pick as their friends. I don't want them to—"

"What? Want them to what?"

"Everyone says you're a smart guy, Albert, so you work it out if ya can."

"You don't want them to play with me because of this." He pointed to the inside of his arm, dragged his index finger along it, then grabbed a handful of skin. His voice trembled with anger, but it never raised in volume. "What's the matter, worried it might rub off on them? That if your kids spend enough time with a darkie or a boong then they might become one too? Is that it?"

There was a pause, and the tension thundered through it. "Peter! Darren! Get in the car and don't muck around. We're goin' home."

"So they can watch me play but not kick the footy with me after, hey? Hey?"

"That's not for me to say now, is it?" The alcohol in her voice was dragging her words together. "Just kick the fucken footy straight, and play well next weekend, all right? Then you can whinge your arse off, while I forget this ever fucken happened."

With that, she turned on her heel and stumbled for her chair, grabbing it and throwing it in the back of the truck her husband was ready to drive away. The other adults disappeared into their cars, obviously supporting the argument that had taken place—a few had been nodding, and the crossed arms and raised chins that had pointed towards Albert gave silent blessing to the woman's chorus.

Albert grabbed the footy and kicked it as hard as he could in the direction of the cars that were making their way around the ground towards the gates. The ball cannoned into the back of one of them—it slowed, then sped up again. Tom heard a cackle come out of the open windows and a string of swearing and insults escape one of the parent's mouths. They quickly made their way out of the gates, leaving Tom and Albert as the only people still there.

Tom silently made his way towards Albert; as he did, the lights that had bathed the field were shut off, and the two found themselves in darkness. Albert looked at Tom and spat, not at him, but near enough, and stormed past him without uttering anything. In Tom's mind it was lucky, because in his surprise and stupor, he would not have had any idea of what to say.

CHAPTER 02

SUNDAY

The beam of light that snuck in between the blind and his window arrived late that morning. Tom rolled over and looked at his clock. It was after nine, and his immediate reaction was to smile, then roll back over and try to go back to sleep. He started to drift, hoping he could get back into the dream he had just left, but then a scarring image invaded his conscious mind—a drunk white woman, screaming abuse at an Aboriginal child with a footy in his hand. Once it was there it was impossible to remove, and he lay on his back, staring at the North Melbourne posters on his wall and the stain on the ceiling that was directly above his head.

When he had arrived home the night before, he had not really believed what had transpired. Chasing after Albert had been almost impossible—he wouldn't stop, wouldn't speak; he hardly even acknowledged Tom's attempts to thwart him, such was his fury. Tom eventually gave up when they got to the top of Albert's street—he had watched Albert storm into his well-kept, sprawling, single-storey house, almost ripping the screen door off the hinges and slamming the front door behind him. Tom had stayed to see if he would come back out, but there was no sign of anything besides a few lights being turned on and off.

He had got home about thirty minutes later and had not known what to say to his mother. Jenny often, out of human interest more than with a hope of solving problems, tried to read her son's moods and vagaries, but realised she had no way of tracking into what was happening in her son's mind, so hadn't tried. She had thought it was football related, and that by the morning, things would be settled and her son would have regained his composure and perspective.

He hadn't. Tom had never seen anything like what had gone on before, in not only the nine months he had lived in Duneldin, but throughout the rest of his life. Of course, he knew about racism—they studied books that dealt with it in English and his mother had spent hours talking to him about the Civil Rights movement in the US and had made him sit through Martin Luther King's 'I Have A Dream' speech on the stereo ("The metaphors, Tom, the metaphors!") but to see it as clearly and as evident as he had the night before had shocked him.

He wondered if Albert had overreacted to what had taken place, but soon realised that he couldn't really judge—his mother had always said when you're part of the dominant race, you can't make a call on what's racist, and only now he really started to appreciate that. He swung his legs out from under the doona and put both feet onto the floor, scrunching his toes into the threadbare carpet. He did a quick check of his legs and feet for soreness from yesterday's game, and gingerly felt a spot on his left arm. It was where he had been knocked while shepherding during the last quarter, and the harder he poked the spot the more it hurt. He took off his pyjama shirt to look at it, but couldn't really see anything, so because there was no evidence of a real injury, he ignored it. He stood up, felt the normal stiffness he felt after he had played, and stumbled down the hallway to the kitchen.

His mother sat at the table, and looked up over her glasses at him. "Hello, there. How are we this morning?"

"We're okay, we think. A bit sore, but all right. Think I might end up with a bruise on my arm, but it feels okay. How are we?"

"We're good too. Quiet day, not too many complaints about what came out yesterday, and we didn't find any mistakes, so we're happy." Jenny paused. "Are we calmer than what we were last night? It seemed like we were rather upset about something."

"Um, yeah. Well …"

"Well?"

"Oh, it's nothing, don't worry about it. It'll be fine."

"Come on, it didn't seem fine when you came in last night. You had your own personal thunderstorm smashing itself apart over your head. Are you all right?"

"Yeah, yeah, I'm fine. It's just …" He paused, not really knowing what to say, or where to begin. "It's really fine. I'm okay, I'm not in trouble, I'll be right to play next week."

Jenny knew her son was lying, but she let it slide. She had made the decision a few years ago that he needed to be treated like a man if she was expecting him to live like one, so when Tom was halfway through his fourteenth year she stopped thinking of him like a child or an adolescent, and started talking to him the way she would talk to a peer. At times she questioned this judgement, but more often than not Tom made decisions that Jenny was secretly proud of, justifying in her mind her decision to speed up the ageing of her son.

"Ah, yes, the big game. How are you feeling about it?"

"Good, I guess. Nowhere as good as what the rest of the town is—I think it's the biggest thing that's happened here for years."

"'It's ten years since the town of Duneldin have had the chance to celebrate Grand Final glory and 17 years since the town has seen any silverware, but thanks to three goals from full forward Jason Turnbull and some brilliant play from Albert Edwards, the town will get an opportunity this Saturday against Masterton at Civic Park Hormiton.' It's the front-page article I'm already drafting up here." She pointed to her forehead, and smiled.

"Masterton!"

"Yep. Came through last night when you were asleep. Apparently they got over the line against Inglewood in a boil over. Jumped them in the first quarter with a strong wind that died and hung on by five points at the end. Inglewood had a chance to tie it in the last few seconds but an impossible shot at goal proved to be, indeed, impossible."

Tom was genuinely surprised. The talk in the change room after their final was that they would be playing Inglewood— the two teams had been clearly beyond the rest of the opposition for the year, and a Grand Final seemed an inevitability.

"Do you know anything else? Any injuries? Who played well? I bet that number 9 played out of his skin."

"Sorry, I don't know anything. I'm hoping to get something from them during the day today that I'll turn into something to go on the inside back page, but at the moment, I'm going to be spending hours working out how to cram everything I have to about the Bombers into two editions. I might even have to run a third, such will be the interest."

"What? You too?"

"What do you mean?"

"You're going to be pushing the Grand Final all week? Fitz warned us last night that it was going to be a huge week and that everyone would be talking about it, and now you're going to be pestering me too. I thought home would be a place I could avoid it all. Aaargh!"

"I won't pester you, but I will expect a few exclusives. Anyone injured yesterday?"

Tom sat mute. Jenny looked at him expectantly.

"Well?"

"Are you serious? Mum, I haven't even had my cereal and you're grilling me already. Be like a real journo. Go and stand on the front step and yell irrelevant questions at me and I'll come out in my jocks and throw something at you."

It was Jenny's job that had brought them to Duneldin. She had been at university studying to be a journalist when she had fallen pregnant with Tom, which threw every one of her plans off track. Instead of heading to a major newspaper and a successful career—as she and her peers had expected her to—she had been forced to take freelance work that fitted in with the life of a mother who had no real support and a family that offered minimal help while criticising her behind her back. Her life had been a challenge, but as Tom had grown older she had been able to take on more, and by the time he had started high school she was able to think seriously about beginning the career that had so far eluded her.

She had met with an old friend to talk about what she might be able to do, and within three weeks, the friend had reached out to a contact in a country newspaper chain to see if she could get her a job. Three weeks after that she was called by an editor in Ballarat who wanted her to work on the *Duneldin Herald*. There had been some rushed conversations with Tom who had realised how excited his mother was and how likely the move would be, and what that would mean for him in the short term. They agreed he would definitely return to Melbourne to study when he finished school, even if she stayed.

Jenny's initial glee at the opportunity to have a full-time, well-paid job at a newspaper was soon qualified. As part of the interview process, she sent some of her work to the editors who were impressed with her ability, and then a phone interview had taken place. When it came to asking her own questions, Jenny only had one. "So, how many other journos will there be?"

There had been a pause on the other end of the line. "The only other people in the office will be the two ladies who do the classifieds. They'll make about the same amount as you and if we're lucky they'll fill more of the paper. As for other journos, you're it."

Jenny had laughed, expecting this to be some kind of joke, but she realised it was true. She rang around other papers the same size and heard the same story—one journo, four, eight or twelve pages depending on what was happening and how many ads got sold, contacts hard to get but once they were found they were like gold, and that it was challenging but satisfying work.

Jenny asked the editor to send her a copy of the paper before she made her mind up. When it arrived she was pleasantly surprised by the professionalism of the layout, the quality of the photographs on the front page, and then inside, how much was going on in the town, but also how much seemed to be getting done by the one journalist—there were at least three articles on each page, and only one byline, and that appeared on the front page. It would be a new world, but one that excited her, and after a series of discussions with Tom—who had seemed to grasp why his mother wanted to leave Melbourne but perhaps didn't understand the true extent of the change—they had accepted. Three weeks later the house was let, the truck was loaded and they had arrived in Duneldin.

Jenny's first day had indeed been eventful. The editor had made the journey out from Ballarat—a rare occurrence, it turned out—and had met Jenny out the front of the newspaper's office, a small, single-doored shopfront with the masthead of the newspaper on the frosted glass. A young man also met them there, who Jenny soon learned was the journalist she was taking over from. He was a young, gaunt and intense man called Anthony, and he was to show her around for the first few days, then would take a position at a larger newspaper in Newcastle. He was obviously ready for the move—his house was completely packed up even though he had two days officially until he left, and his introductions and explanations were perfunctory at best. He made passing comments about who the best people were to talk to in the town and made efforts to introduce her around, but there was an obvious wall between the old and the new in terms of who would talk. Jenny had tried to be gracious and humble towards Anthony, but she wondered if they had both realised that they were going in different directions and knew it. Anthony would be heading to a move up the ladder, while she was happily starting out on a career that had seemed a long way away for a long time, but now seemed like a thing she could believe in.

Tom had finished his breakfast and was rinsing his dishes in the sink, looking out the window at the empty backyard that had been designed to have kids running around, but now contained three pot plants and grass that was screaming out to be mowed. He didn't look over his shoulder, but asked his mother, "Mum, do you ever have to report on something that makes you feel sick?"

This conversation had taken place in different forms before, but Jenny sensed that there was more to it this time.

"I haven't really had to since I got here, but yes, of course I do. Any journalist does but I don't let the sickness cloud my writing, or my place."

"What if it's so bad that you can't help it? Have you ever had stories that have been so bad you want to write opinion pieces and not just reports?"

"Sometimes when I wrote about politics I was expected to take a side, but I hated it—I'm only meant to be an observer who reports on facts. When I was working freelance and was desperate, if the editors wanted me to write something that I didn't want to, I just dug around and made enough phone calls until I could get someone to say what the editors wanted me to say on the record, and I could convince myself that I didn't really write it. I never felt good about it but it's all I could do. What's happening?"

"Have you ever felt like it since we moved?"

"Don't answer a question with a question, it's bad rhetoric. What happened?"

Tom turned around and looked at his mother with his arms crossed. "You're avoiding. Have you ever felt like you had to do it here?"

"You're avoiding too." They looked at each other for a moment, almost daring the other to crack. Jenny realised she would need to speak first so she could ask the questions he needed her to, but Tom blurted out.

"They're not as open-minded here, are they? The people, I mean. They're still hanging on to some real old-school values."

"Hmm. Old-school values? You mean like going to church on a Sunday and only driving Australian cars?"

"No, I mean in the way they treat people. I mean, we learn about discrimination at school and we read the right books and stuff, but there's still a sense of …" Jenny knew exactly what he was going to say, and finished his sentence for him.

"Of us being different to them."

"Yeah, that's it. I thought I had started to understand the town and felt like it was a fair and safe place to live, but now I feel like I've just been missing everything that goes on."

"What happened?"

Tom paused, ensuring he had the picture right in his mind. "I was with Albert yesterday, and some drunk woman gave him an earful about not playing with her kids because he's Aboriginal."

"Really? How drunk was she?"

"Drunk, but not so drunk that you'd excuse the way she spoke to him. It was so direct and brutal." Tom paused. "You should have seen him. He was so angry it looked as if the fury was going to actually leak out of him."

"Did you talk to him about it?"

"I wanted to, but he wasn't listening to anything. He stormed home, and I couldn't stop him."

"Who was the woman?"

"I'd never seen her before. She said her name was Thorpe. Had two kids."

"Jane Thorpe? Middle-length blondish hair, heavyset and about my height?"

"That's her."

"Yeah, I've met her once or twice. She works for the stock trader on Commercial Road. I've had to ask her for some numbers a couple of times when the trades happen. She seems all right— I mean, just a low-level hayseed, but that describes the majority of the town. Nothing offensive."

"You wouldn't have known it hearing her speak. It's like she'd never heard of equality or civil rights. Jesus, Mum. It's 1992! I thought everyone was moving past that kind of crap after Mabo and the Royal Commission. The worst thing was that she told Albert not to worry about her being a racist, just that he needed to kick straight."

"Honestly?" A look of surprise crossed Jenny's face. "She said that?"

"Yep. And there were about ten other adults behind her who agreed with what she had to say."

"Did you say anything to her?"

"What?"

"Did you tell her to shut up or say anything to support Albert?"

"What?" Tom, for the first time, thought about his role in what had happened. "No; I mean, it happened so fast, I just ..." His voice trailed away. "What should I have done?"

"It's hard to say. When you're in shock, sometimes the world slows down, sometimes it speeds up. Did you want to say anything?" She looked at him with a raised eyebrow.

Tom ran his hand through his hair and across his face. "Not until now. Jesus. What will he be thinking?"

"Hard to say. Do you want to find out?"

"Yes. No. Oh, shit." Tom looked lost, and his mother didn't know how to guide him. She paused. Tom sat down opposite her and asked, "You gonna write about it in the paper?"

Jenny looked at her son and sighed. "No, Tom, not if I want to keep my job."

Tom's mind was still racing from all that had happened. He didn't know what he should do, but he knew that sitting and stewing wasn't going to solve anything.

"I'm going for a ride. I'll be back around lunch," he said.

Jenny hardly looked up when she replied, "'Kay. Wear a helmet," then went back to her book. Tom smiled at her obsession with reading and how she used it to take her away from her actual life, even after the conversation they had just finished, and walked out the front door.

The morning was overcast, but the sky was hardly threatening. Tom walked to the garage, opened the side door and went into the darkness. There was enough light to find his bike and the helmet, and without really thinking about it he threw his leg over the crossbar, found the pedals and was off.

He often used the bike as a respite—the town was so flat that he could ride for hours and not really get tired, and there had been times when he had been trying to find his feet as the new kid that had seen him ride around aimlessly, looking for signs that he belonged. This time he knew where he was heading—down Main Road, across the creek and to Albert's house. He didn't think he would talk to him, but just by riding in the neighbourhood he felt like he would be giving his support to a cause that he didn't even know existed the day before.

Tom tried to think of other times where he hadn't registered the undercurrent that had been exposed last night, and it didn't take him long. The town had a notable Aboriginal community, and while Tom had always believed that everyone got along well, he realised that he had been ignorant.

His naivety was born in the classrooms in cities where he hadn't been directly exposed to racial differences. The teachers at his school had taught them that racism was something that had happened once but now, thanks to Harper Lee, the Bicentennial, and a couple of months ago a man called Eddie Mabo, it was a thing that was dying.

He acknowledged how narrow his vision had been. There had been looks at the supermarket when the Aboriginal families were in line to buy groceries, the way the barman at the town's main pub had always served the white customers first, and even the way the Aboriginal community lived in pretty much the same quadrant of town, regardless of where they worked and how much money they had.

When he first arrived Tom had thought that had happened by choice, but now he wondered if the town had created a ghetto for the Aboriginal population, and it was simpler for them to live where they would be racially welcomed, instead of living in the parts of town they actually wanted to live in. He also recognised that he knew a lot more about certain Aboriginal families than others—the families that were part of the sporting clubs, went to parents' nights at the school and nodded their hellos as they walked down Scott Street against those who he had never known, and in his own way, turned his eyes away from. He had felt like every Aboriginal in the town was the same, but by doing so, sent a message that it was okay to feel this way, and that therefore, all the white people were the same. He now realised how untrue all of this had become.

As all this had gone through his head and dread had descended on him, he found himself on Albert's street. He had been here many times, and even been welcomed inside Albert's home, but now he felt like an outsider, and someone who was not wanted. He rode past Albert's house quickly, not really looking at the front door, but his glance revealed that Albert's bedroom curtains were still drawn. There weren't many signs of life, besides the family cars parked in the garage, and the scooters and skateboards left on the front lawn. Tom felt relieved, and as he came to the end of the street and faced an intersection, he felt his legs loosen. He finally sat down in the seat, and started pedalling for the main street, hoping to find a friendly face so he could have a conversation about anything but football.

His sense of relief was cut short. The way to the centre of town was fairly direct when on a bike, and Tom cut through two small streets and a park to head there and made his way down a court that led to the back of the supermarket car park. He was part daydreaming as he rode, but he was soon forced to regain his focus. As he pedalled towards the end of the cul-de-sac, he saw Albert speaking intensely to a group of boys, all of whom he recognised from his football team, and all Indigenous.

Albert was laughing out loud when one of the boys nudged him and pointed at Tom riding towards them. Albert turned, and seeing Tom, looked back at the group, and said something low, so that Tom couldn't hear it. Tom cruised towards them, doing everything he could to relax and not feel nervous—he had no idea why he should feel concerned about talking to a group of boys who yesterday he had been hugging and high-fiving, but seeing Albert made him feel as if there was something that had changed between them. He had not really connected with any of the other boys in the same way he had with Albert, but even so, he could not explain the sense of anxiety he felt as he slowed to chat with them. He got off the bike, and walked towards them, unbuckling his helmet.

"Lads, how are we? Everyone recovered?"

Albert made it clear from his first sentence that the conversation was his, and that he would control it. "Brudda. Recovered from what?"

"Oh, you know, the bumps, bruises and scratches."

"You mean the lovely chat I had with Mrs Thorpe?"

Tom looked down, then back at the group who now loosely stood behind Albert, the obvious leader. "Um, yeah, that too." Tom tried to laugh, but it stuck in his throat.

Albert's gaze drilled into Tom, and Tom could recognise the anger that was behind it. Albert said with disdain, "I was just trying to tell the boys what happened, but I'm not sure if I got my facts straight. What do you remember from last night?"

"What?" Tom was taken aback by the request, and his mind was scrambling. "Oh, look, a bunch of pissed people were acting like dickheads, and one of them took the prize for being the biggest idiot in the town. I don't think—"

"Brudda, I haven't been able to do much but think. This is how I remember what happened, but I don't want to miss any of the details. Tell me if I get anything wrong, won't you? A pissed white woman who was supported by about ten other pissed white people told me that it was okay to play footy well and that I should help the town win a Premiership, but that I wasn't good enough to have a kick with her soon-to-be racist children. And this was after I had tried to let you know quietly that I didn't want to have anything to do with her kids. Sound right?"

"Look, Albert, she's a dickhead. A pissed dickhead, who has no idea about what comes out of her mouth. What she says doesn't mean anything, and she's only speaking for her own ignorance. Surely you can see that."

"What I can see is that you haven't ever sat on this side of what comes out of those kinds of mouths, and I'm not sure who you think you're speaking for. Did you notice how many families there were sitting behind her, and what that means? There were about three different clans there, and they're big and they spread out across the whole town. You haven't been here long enough to see how long this has been going on. I tried to warn you."

"Warn me? What does that mean? And been here long enough? You don't need to be in a town for years to realise that there are a few people who still believe in a bullshit idea that died out years ago."

Behind Albert, Tom heard words like "few" and "died out" spat back at him. Tom felt the sweat starting to roll down his back, even though he knew it was cold. Beatsy, one of the tallest of the group, threw his head back and snorted a laugh. "Mate," Beatsy said, and it was one of the only times he had directly addressed Tom. "I know you're in the top maths class at school, but you need to think about how many a few is. You mean a small amount? A middle-sized number? A metric shedload? You need to look closely at the town and how it works. Have you ever even thought about why Albert isn't the captain of the team? Have ya? Are there better players? Smarter players? Better leaders? You've been on the field when we play. Do you white fellas know more about where to run or who to kick it to than we do, or is there another reason why there aren't any captains, vice captains with this skin?"

Tom stared at Beatsy, mouth half open. He looked at the other boys who were part of the group and felt like he'd been punched in the stomach and was winded. He'd never even thought about the captain's position—he just figured that the coach had picked a kid, any kid, at the start of a season years ago and that he'd never felt the need to change it.

"What can we do about it?"

"We?" Albert laughed incredulously. "Why do you think we"—indicating the group around him—"would want or need your help? What would your white self suggest? Not ride the bus? Have a sit in? Get all the Aborigines in the town to walk down the main street and protest, hoping the paper writes about it and then wait for the civil rights leaders to show up? We're not going to do anything. We're just going to go on putting up with this shit until we get a chance to leave the town and never come back."

He paused, and looked over his shoulder at the group, then turned around with a smile on his face that Tom knew wasn't real. "Or maybe we'll do something else. Who knows? How about you put your safety helmet back on and keep going. We'd love to stay and chat but I'm not sure you would want to hear what we have to say. See you at school tomorrow." Tom watched as Albert turned his back on him, an act of dismissal Tom acknowledged was what he deserved.

As Tom slowly rode into town—his helmet hanging loosely over the handlebars in an act of defiance he couldn't explain—he thought about his friendship with Albert, and why the contempt he had faced just minutes ago dug into him so much.

The first time they had met Albert was carrying a football— even though it was the first week of February—into a class they had once a fortnight called Personal Directions. It was where they got a chance to sit around and, it seemed, do even less than they did in some of their other classes. Their teacher was Mr Hills, who, like all the teachers in the school, had gained a basic nickname, Hillsy. He took them through a weird combination of career discussions, ethics questions and even first aid, which Tom soon realized Hillsy had no qualification to teach. Albert spent most of the lesson trying to disrupt the class by asking challenging ethical questions that Hillsy couldn't help but be dragged into, and Tom admired Albert's ability to word the questions in a way that the rest of the class tuned into, if only to see how Hillsy would answer and maintain his dignity.

"Sir, hypothetically, if I was to get a girl pregnant, would I legally be required to stick around and look after her?"

"Sir, hypothetically, if I was to see an elderly lady drop a winning lottery ticket on the street and she didn't notice, am I expected to give it back to her?"

"Sir, when was the last time you knowingly broke the law but didn't feel like you were really doing the wrong thing?"

And on they went. In the first two lessons, Tom, as a new student, was just trying to fit in and keep his head down. By the third, when he realised that he had to try to fit in or spend the rest of the year in limbo, he started engaging with the lessons, and the questions. They were the kind of things he had begun to ask his mother, and given her open-minded belief in his development, she answered as truthfully as she could, which gave Tom an insight many of his peers were yet to discover.

The third lesson of Personal Directions was on managing money, and Hillsy was trying to explain how interest worked. Albert languidly put his hand up while Hilly was doing basic maths on the board, and asked, "But, Hillsy, why give it such a stupid name? Why would anyone be interested in paying it?"

"Well, that's a good question, Albert. Perhaps you could think about it ... Yes, Tom?" Tom had raised his hand, and the class looked at him.

"Would it be because the banks are only interested in ripping us off?"

Albert quickly followed, "Or perhaps they're interested in their own profits and not caring how they get them?"

"Or maybe they see our interest in not paying it?"

"Or they're only interested in finding out how much irony we can deal with." Tom and Albert looked at each other, and smiled; Hillsy looked at them both, and to no-one in particular said, "And so we see two kindred spirits meet. I wondered how long it would take."

When the bell went the students left the class quickly, and Albert and Tom found themselves walking down the hall together to their next class. Tom looked at Albert and offered his hand. "Hey, I'm new here. My name's Tom."

Albert looked sideways at him, and at his outstretched hand. "I know, brudda. We all know who you are and what your name is. Most of us even know where you live." Albert looked at him. "Something else?"

"Yeah. Well, usually when someone introduces themselves, the other person does the same thing."

"Really? No shit. Brother, what's my name?"

"Um, well, Albert."

"So you already knew. What happens next? Do I need to present my card or something?"

"No, but, you know, I just thought …"

"Don't worry. I know who you are. You know who I am. Let's just take it from there, okay? The bigger question is though, can you kick with both feet?"

"What? Both feet? Oh, um, yeah, actually. My first coach made us kick on the opposite side when we were just learning to kick, so it kind of became natural."

"Smart man. Do you know when training starts?"

"No idea. It's only February. When does the season start?"

"April, but training starts in two weeks. Hopefully you and both your feet can make it. Here we are."

Tom looked up, and saw he was standing outside his English class. "Have fun, brudda. *Macbeth* awaits." Albert raised his arms and looked to the roof. *"I have given suck, and know what it is to feed the babe that milks me. I would, while it was smiling in my face, have plucked my nipple from his boneless gums, and dashed the brains out, had I so sworn as you have done to this."* Albert was up in Tom's face, eyes wide and angry, his hair flopping in his face. In an instant, he stood back and laughed. "Man, that Lady Macbeth's a nut."

Tom was openly impressed. A couple of people had noticed Albert's performance and were laughing at him. "How can you do that?"

"What, quote the play? It's easy, brudda. You just read it."

From then on, the two boys had developed a laidback relationship—they didn't necessarily seek each other out, but when they did, there was a comfort in intelligence and manner that Tom enjoyed. Albert was respected around the school thanks to his sporting prowess, and Tom's association with him, however stretched, helped him to move through the social circles in the school easily. Tom was always the new kid, but Albert's familiarity helped the label to be rubbed off him fairly quickly.

As the year had progressed and Tom's other friendships had developed, he always looked to the connection he had with Albert as a key part of his new experience, but the events on the night of the semi-final now slapped his perception out of focus. Would Albert now see him as just another white kid who was protected by his impenetrable skin? He hoped not. He knew that somehow he would have to do something to prove it otherwise. He wondered if his mother would be able to help him, but doubted her and her need to see the world objectively. He knew that school on Monday would be a strange double world—the kids would be filled with excitement about the Grand Final, but Albert and his reaction would inevitably dominate Tom's thinking. As he pedalled home to lunch and the rest of his day doing homework and listening to music, he tried to plan how he would treat the next few days, but his thinking ended up being an empty series of quips and deflection. If only it was going to be that easy.

CHAPTER 03

MONDAY

Tom's first thought when he woke up involved a grunt, and an unconscious movement towards the top of his left arm—it was more tender than it had been the day before, and now when he prodded it with a single finger there was enough pain for it to be alarming. It wasn't impossible to move or to swing himself out of bed, but he still realised he would be aware of it the rest of the day, and when he threw the covers off, he knew he would have to favour it. He realised he should have probably paid more attention to it the day before, but his brain had not been able to slow down enough to think about much else.

His mother had again quizzed him about what, in her words, was doing drunken laps around his head, and he had tried to explain. Again, she had counselled him to just be himself and, in his own way, to keep his head down. He didn't really know what that meant or how he was supposed to do it, given that there would be two stories running the whole week at school—one was the obvious and shiny one, about how the town might finally have some football glory to celebrate, and the unknown and bleaker one, about how there would be a group of boys in the team who would never really feel the sense of jubilation everyone hoped for.

Normally Tom rode to school, but for some reason today he decided to walk, which meant that he would have to leave early. He made his lunch quickly—same as always: ham, cheese and tomato sandwich, banana, and a muesli bar—grabbed some coins from his desk to spend at the canteen and then shoved everything else he needed into his bag. As he slung it over his shoulder and made for the door, he yelled "See ya, Mum!" to the shower door and received a muffled reply.

Making his way through the school gates, Tom immediately sensed that it would be a different week. Over the entrance to the school, in the red and black club colours, someone had draped a sign that screamed 'Bombers for Premiers!!!'. There were streamers hanging from the door to the administration office. Kids he only knew by sight were now nodding at him, and he received pats on the back from people he could never remember having contact with. As he made his way to his locker to put his bag away, he tried to keep his head down—literally—not knowing how to deal with what he assumed was low-level fame. Happily, when he got to the row of metallic boxes that passed for lockers in the school, he saw Samantha Green, who was slowly shaking her head at him. "Ooooh, Tom," she crooned. "You're my hero."

Samantha, or, as she told everyone to call her, Manny, had been the person who had first made the effort to speak to Tom when he had arrived. Their friendship had struck up quickly, based on a handful of things—music tastes, books, and the fact that they both had arrived recently in the town and knew they probably wouldn't be there much longer after they finished high school. Tom had always found her attractive—medium-length brown hair, newly straightened teeth and round brown eyes, and he liked the way her nose scrunched when she smiled or how she could roll her eyes better than anyone he'd ever met. Manny's family had moved to the town the year before—like Tom's own situation, her family had relocated for work, and she hadn't been too happy about it. Her father was an engineer who had been appointed to a senior position in the gold mine that existed about 150 km from the town, and he spent most of his nights living on site and came home for the weekends, which left Manny, her mother and younger sister sitting at home in a town they knew they could get relocated from without much notice. Manny had a sharp wit and a more-than-healthy level of cynicism, and she and Tom spent a lot of time together trying to make themselves laugh at each other's expense.

"If I was your hero, I'd say you've finally starting taking those pills everyone's been raving about," Tom replied, smiling.

"Oh no, this is real. Our class, our whole year level, the whole school, the whole town is frothing with excitement about you guys winning on Saturday. Tom!" And here her words began to drip with the sarcasm Tom was used to. "If you win, you might actually cure cancer!"

"Yes, Manny, that's right. We score more points than they do, and everyone's life will immediately become better. Even yours. You'll finally be able to get the personality transplant that you so desperately need."

Manny's reaction was the one that acknowledged a win: she showed Tom her elegantly shaped middle finger, and then started to load her books from her bag to her locker. "How does it actually feel?"

Tom had been hoping she would ask a serious question so he could answer seriously, and he took this as the closest thing he might get. "It felt good for about an hour, then it didn't."

"Why not?"

"'Cos I saw something that made winning and losing irrelevant. Albert got screamed at by a drunk woman for playing footy with her kids—she said it was okay for him to play for the town's team and win, but not okay to play kick to kick with a couple of eight-year-olds."

"I don't get it. Why can't he play with them?"

"Colour of his skin."

"No." Manny's tone expressed her disbelief.

"Yep. I wouldn't have believed it either, but there it was. You should have heard her. There were about fifteen people behind her as well, all laughing at her and leering at him. All of a sudden the excitement of being in a Grand Final that we should probably win easily died off."

There was a pause, while both of them looked away from each other, deep in thought. Tom brought his eyes back to Manny's face and saw resignation. It wasn't what he expected.

"What?"

"What do you mean what? It's unbelievable, but it is what it is. Do you think Albert will do anything about it? Can he do anything about it?" She was leaning with her back against her locker, scanning the corridors.

"I don't know, but I saw him yesterday with the other Aboriginal guys from the team, and they were furious."

"Of course they were, but what will they do? This won't be over, and it's probably not the first time something like this has happened to him. Albert is way too intense to let it go."

"I don't know. There's something up, but they wouldn't tell me. I don't know if Albert blames me for not sticking up for him."

"Did you?"

"No, there wasn't time. I should have told her to shut up, or get stuffed, or something, but I was too shocked."

"I don't reckon he'll be angry at you for doing nothing; he's probably gonna be more angry at the whole town for it happening at all."

"I want to do something to let him know what I thought of it, but I don't know what."

Manny sighed, and put her hand on Tom's arm. Tom looked at her, surprised.

"I know it's a big deal," she said, "but what are you going to do? This is one of those towns. There's a surface, then there's underneath the surface, and you got to see underneath. You can't be that surprised. You could do something in your own way, get into a rage, and for five minutes people will remember it, then the surface will cover over again, and nothing will change. These places have this kind of thing rusted on to them. I know it. You know it. You've seen it. How many Aboriginal people work in the office at the club?"

Tom paused. "What? What does that have to do with it?"

"It has a lot to do with it. How many Aboriginal people work in the office?"

"None that I can remember."

"How many of the groundsmen are Aboriginal? How many are on the committee? How many Aboriginal people are there on the Wall of Honour that recognises service to the wonderful Duneldin football team?"

"Yep. Got it."

"Think about this though, Tom. How many Aboriginal stories does your mum write about in the paper?" Tom started to respond, but he was cut off. "I know she's not a moron, but a lot of the people who read the paper are. She's not ignorant, she knows her audience. You think there aren't things happening in the Aboriginal community that people shouldn't know about? Come on. Not even you are that dumb."

"Maybe I am that dumb. Hell, it's everywhere. When did you notice?"

"How many black girls get made captain of the netball team, do you reckon? Last year when I turned up for my first training session, and after they stopped laughing at the fact I couldn't really catch or throw, the Aboriginal kids were the first to come and say hello. The others did too, and not long after they did, they told me to be careful of the Aboriginal girls and not get too close to them. They never explained why. Then I noticed all the white kids got the good positions and the Aboriginal girls got the worst ones or got put on the bench—and the Aboriginal girls never complained, they just played, and we were good because of them."

"Is it the same this year?"

"Jesus. You are ignorant. Have I talked about the netball team this year? Have you seen me heading to training? Have I come in with busted knees and ankles like all the other girls? I stopped playing."

"Because of the stupidity?"

"No, because I was shit! There are only so many times when Meghan O'Rourke throws the ball at you and you get whacked in the face before you decide you aren't cut out for it. I still get invited to help out every once in a while, but I make sure I'm busy doing something else."

Tom laughed at her again and had a brief moment of appreciation of their friendship. He had never felt that she would lie to him or try to be anything more than a friend he could absolutely rely on.

Sometimes he had wondered what it would be like to kiss her, but every time he did he shook his head with the knowledge that it could mean the end of the most significant relationship he had in the town. At a party in July, a group of kids from their year level had forced the two of them into a shed with the hope that 'something would happen' and it did—Tom won scissors rock paper in the dark 10 – 8, and then they were let out, much to the disappointment of those who were hoping they would have something to talk about the following morning.

Over her shoulder he saw a couple of the boys from the team walking to class, and they had a crew of hangers-on a few steps behind them, talking excitedly. It brought him back to the good and bad of what would happen that day, and the rest of the week. "I can't ignore it, and I know something is up, but what do I do? Dob them in? Who to? Not play out of protest? Write a letter to the paper?"

Manny laughed at this, but then she looked at Tom and saw the confusion in his face and again she reached out to him. The bell for first period went, and without thinking they moved off to their first class.

They walked together until the end of the corridor, when they went their separate ways. Before they did, she grabbed his pencil case, slowly turning him towards her. "Look, Atticus, think about what you can achieve by raging about it. Maybe you can do something, maybe you can't. What you will do is make it difficult for everyone. This town is stuck inside the view it created for itself 30 years ago, before Aboriginals were even able to vote, and you turning up as some open-minded city slicker who is still cutting their teeth on the town. Trying to tell them what to do won't help, mostly because we both know we're leaving here as soon as we finish high school. Right? I'd leave it with Albert. God knows he understands the way things work, and he'll have a plan."

"Think I should talk to him?"

"Sure, but don't expect to like what you hear."

As Tom walked to twentieth-century history, he was hung up on the idea that Albert had a plan. He knew that something would happen, and that the Aboriginal boys were up to something, but all of the ideas he had in his head ended up with a fight of some kind. He knew Albert wasn't that dumb. One of the first things he realised about Albert was that he was smart, and he read everything he could get his hands on, and that he knew how to apply what he learned. Tom didn't think Albert would be dumb enough to try to take what happened on front on.

In history, they had been learning about the Vietnam War, and the way it had been completely different to anything that Australia or America had fought before. His teacher, Mr Shepherd, was a quick-witted and genuinely funny man who made history live in his classroom. He was always recreating battles and trying to give the students a real appreciation of what had taken place hundreds of years beforehand, and the kids in his class still recalled with wonder some of the lessons on World War One, particularly where they had all been given a shovel and some hessian sacks and told to go out to the oval and start digging a trench. They had incredulously followed instructions and were only stopped when the groundsman stormed out from his shed and started yelling at them for destroying school property. Shep—as everyone, including his wife, called him—hadn't thought to check with anyone about his lesson, he just went ahead and did it anyway. The trench activity had been followed up by sitting in class for a full fifty minutes with their feet in buckets of muddy water so they could understand trench foot, and there had been some sharp letters back from parents about the conditions of shoes and feet the next morning. As he always did, the teacher responded with, "Well, at least we're all learning something," which was his explanation for everything.

Tom walked into class, and took his regular seat near the window, three quarters of the way back into the room. He called it the half back flank of the class. It was where he tried to sit every lesson. Albert followed him soon after, and only greeted him with a nod and a half-smirk, before plopping down two seats across from him. Tom wanted to lean over and talk to him, but before he really got the chance, Shep burst into the class, barking orders, as he normally did.

"Right. Everyone take an eraser or a pen out of your pencil case, and put it on the desk in front of you. Right. Done that? What? Elizabeth, come on, get with it. And O'Farrell, stop daydreaming about what will happen this weekend—you need to understand the past before you can think about the future, son. And Tom!"

Tom quickly looked away from Albert and to the front, worried about what would become of him. "Yes, Shep?"

"Nothing. Just seeing if you were paying attention. Right. Has everyone got something relatively inoffensive in their hands? Good. Today we're talking about the Viet Cong and the way they fought their war. Last week we learned about the Americans and saturation bombing and how useless that was, today we're going to see the way that a smaller, more mobile army was able to take down the biggest fighting force in the world. You see those supposedly inoffensive pieces of stationery you're holding? Good. Every time I turn around to write something on the board or am helping someone, feel free to throw them at me."

There was stunned silence.

"What?" one of the kids eventually asked.

"You heard me. When I'm not looking, I want you to throw something at me. It's how the guerillas worked. They hit the Americans when they didn't know it was coming, and it drove the Yanks crazy." With this, a kid called Marco raised his arm, ready to throw his eraser at his teacher. "Whoa, whoa, whoa, you bloodthirsty scoundrel." Shep smiled. "Here's the rub. If I see anyone actually try to attack me, you'll all get a compulsory 1500-word essay on guerilla tactics."

The students groaned. "That's the other side of the equation. Every time the Americans suspected or found guerillas, they destroyed the villages and infrastructure that supported them. It made being a guerilla really risky, but it also cost the Americans— they were seen as potentially killing innocent victims as a way of winning the war, and that had cost them at home, after the photos of what was happening eventually got onto the front pages of American newspapers. You need to imagine I'm the Americans— if I have evidence of you throwing something, then I'll know where to retaliate, and you'll all cop the punishment for the actions of one person. Got it?" There was a pause as the students nodded. "Good. Now open your books and your textbooks, and head to the chapter we worked on last lesson and keep ploughing through the questions. Game on, everyone."

As the students started their work, Shep moved around the class, nudging kids to get going. Every once in a while, he would take an eraser or pen to the head and back. He almost caught a kid a couple of times, but overall, the students did well. Shep went on to describe in remarkable detail the way that the Viet Cong had been able to attack and demoralize the Americans, and how it led to the slow but eventual victory of the guerillas. As Tom took it all in, and was again amazed at how little he knew about the way the world worked, his eyes fell on Albert, who was sitting ramrod straight, and staring intently at the picture of the guerillas that had been stuck to the board, and not at all noticing anything else that was going on around him. Shep had launched into one of his regular tangential rants about history, this time talking about a place that sounded like Mee Lie, but Albert couldn't have cared less. Tom looked at him and wondered what was going on behind the brightness of his eyes, but knew that he wouldn't ever really find out.

The bell went to end the lesson. Albert got up to go quickly, as did Tom.

Tom had to chase him down the corridor to walk beside him, and when he did, Albert looked at him, and again gave him a nod. "Hey," Tom said. "How ya doin'?"

Albert smiled, and replied, "Great. Wasn't so good, but now? Great."

Tom tried to laugh, but it sounded more like he was choking. "Why, because of My Lai? Nothing great about that."

"No, but the whole lesson made me think. You need to understand the past before you can think about the future, remember?" Tom looked at Albert, and then spoke without thinking.

"Albert, what are you talking about? Ever since Saturday you've been completely weird and acting as if nothing happened and everything happened at the same time. I get that you're shitty and annoyed, but are you at least going to talk to me? I was there when it happened too, you know."

Albert stopped, and whirled on Tom. He moved in so he was almost nose to nose with him, which made Tom take a step back.

"I know you were there, brudda. I've got a good memory. I know you were annoyed, but I didn't hear you saying anything, did I? You were quiet then, so maybe I'm just choosing to be quiet around you now, hey?" There was a fury and a malice in his words that Tom recoiled from.

"But you know I don't buy that bullshit, Albert, we've talked about it. You know I don't."

Albert stepped back, and sighed. "I know you don't, brudda, but don't you get that your silence was really loud?" He paused again, just for a moment. "It's not you, mate, but it is you—it's the way this town works and has worked forever. You don't get it because you've never been on the other side of it. And now, thanks to that"—he jerked a finger over his shoulder towards the classroom they had just walked out of—"I know what I'm going to do."

Tom looked at Albert expectantly, but Albert just smiled. "Well?" Tom said. "What are you going to do?"

"Come on." Albert chuckled. "You wouldn't really expect a guerilla to tell you, would you? That defeats the purpose of the tactic. You'll know when it happens though. See ya, brudda." He turned away from Tom and walked down the hall towards the exit door. He pushed against it, hard, slamming it open and letting a bright light into the corridor that made Tom shield his eyes. By the time they had quickly adjusted, Albert had disappeared.

When the bell went to end the day, Tom quickly emptied his locker, threw his backpack over his back and headed for home. The bruise on his arm had started to throb a bit, and he wanted to get home, rest it and ice it. It had started to get worse through the day, and every time he prodded it in class with the hope it wouldn't hurt anymore, he actually felt the pain increasing.

He didn't think it was so bad that he wouldn't be able to play, but even so, he realised it wasn't a risk worth taking. By the time he got to his street he felt like his bicep was screaming, and he started to worry. He mounted the front steps to his door, unlocked it, and then went to the kitchen to begin his ritual demolishing of whatever his mother had bought on Sunday afternoon.

Two bowls of Weetbix and four pieces of raisin toast later, he sat on the couch with his arm on the top of the couch, a bag of frozen peas inside a tea towel resting on it. He was trying to read the book they were studying in English—yet another classic, this time the one about a group of boys marooned on an island, trying to survive while the world disintegrated around them. As he did, his mind kept wandering back to what had started to happen around him, and each time he came at what he had seen on Saturday and how it had then played out, each path led him to the realisation that he was still very much an outsider in the community, and that for all of his superficial awareness of the town, he really hadn't scratched the exterior of what the town was.

Manny's comments about leaving town as soon as she was old enough to go to the city and study kept ringing in his ears, and he knew that would be his path as well. If it was, why should he care about the small-mindedness of a section of a community that one day he would leave behind? Was it worth trying to be a peacemaker when no peace was ever going to be properly made?

His thought process was broken by the swinging of the screen door that announced the arrival of his mother. She walked into the living room where he was sitting, slung her backpack onto the spare chair, and slumped on to the couch, next to Tom.

"Bloody hell. What a day. From the minute I got there until I locked the door it seemed like it wasn't going to stop. Even the sales girls couldn't believe it. So many phone calls and stories about the goddamned Grand Final. You'd think it was being played at the MCG in front of 100,000 people the way everyone's carrying on. This town has a lot of things going for it, but one thing it doesn't have is perspective." She looked over at him and seemed to notice him for the first time. Then her eyes saw the peas sitting on the top of his arm, and her eyebrows raised. "What's going on? What's with the peas? Are you all right? We're meant to be eating them tonight, you know."

"Hi, Mum, nice to see you too." Tom looked at his mother in a disapproving way, but then smiled. "I'm okay. My arm just has a bit of bruise from Saturday that only seemed to flare up today, so I'm trying to ice it." He paused. "Hey, do you feel like you're a part of this town?"

"What do you mean?"

"I mean, when you walk down the street, do you feel as if you're actually in a place where you belong and where you want to stay?"

"Wow. Can't we do small talk first? Something like *'Gee, Mum, sounds stressful, why don't you tell me about it? Or, Mum, that's awful, let me put the kettle on and you can tell me all about it. Or even, that sounds terrible, Mum, what's for dinner?'* Something like that?"

"Sorry. How's this? That's terrible that your day was so stressful, Mum, why don't you tell me all about it as I stumble over to the kitchen to make you a cup of tea that I'll spill on the way back over to the couch where you're slumped like an alcoholic bag lady thinking about tonight's dinner? How was that?"

"Nice, and so sarcastically caring. After all that, I'll make the tea, thanks. Look, I know what you mean. I feel it too, but what do you expect? We've only been here for a short time, really, and there are people who were born here, have never seriously left, and plan on dying in the house they grew up in. We're a couple of blow-ins who are trying to work out where we fit. I really struggle with it, because I know there are things going on that no-one wants to open up and tell me about, but if I'd been here my whole life, then I'd have a good understanding of them without needing to pry."

"Really? Like what?"

"Well." Jenny paused, wondering how far to open this door, then selecting her words carefully.

"There's a woman who works in the bank who always has bruises on her wrist that she keeps trying to hide by wearing long-sleeve shirts that don't completely cover them. Where do they come from? There's a man who no-one ever speaks to who spends all his time in the TAB putting bets on. Who is he, and where does he get his money? There are kids who ride brand-new bikes down the main street every day but their shoes are worn and their pants are threadbare and covered in patches. What are their parents doing to have that happen? People in the town know the answers, but no-one actually wants to ask the questions."

"How do you notice this stuff?"

"It's part of the job. If you're really good at it, you can get answers to questions by looking at the way people respond as much as what they say. I used to love asking criminals and cheats questions I knew the answer to, then watching how their eyes used to reveal the lies they told. Now I try to do it to the guy who owns the pub, but the lies are worse."

"Worse? Why worse?"

"Because the lies he tells are so personal. A politician lies about how his policies are going to affect millions, so you can't personalise them. Mac at the pub lies about the kids he sells alcohol to, but you see those kids sitting under the war memorial pissed on Saturday afternoon, and you realise how close it is. What made you think about this anyway?"

"Albert. He's planning to do something on Saturday with the other Aboriginal kids, but I don't know what, and he won't tell me. I tried to tell him I was on his side about what happened on Saturday, but he just brushed me off. I spent the whole day watching him, and I know he's up to something."

"Why do you care so much? What can he possibly do?"

"I care because the town cares. Think about it. All the attention you're getting, all the attention I'm getting. Kids pat me on the back who I've never seen before, and even the teachers are dropping references into lessons about what will happen if we win. I can't imagine what it's going to be like if we do win, but the thing that scares me more is how everyone will feel if we lose."

Jenny looked at her son, again, not really knowing how to counsel him. "Look, sometimes in life you realise all you can control is what you have a direct influence over. If Albert is going to do something, then he'll do it. I don't know him all that well, but from the times I've met him, he seems clever and driven—which can be good when everything's going well, but dangerous if it isn't. Look, Tom, does it give it context if I try to tell you it's just a game?"

Tom snorted, and replied, "Are you kidding? If it was just a game, would everyone care this much?"

"Ha! Good point. I'll be in the kitchen, making tea and licking my intellectual wounds. Is a pie okay for dinner? After today, I'd prefer the oven to do most of the cooking."

CHAPTER 04

TUESDAY

Usually, day two was Tom's favourite day at school—he had double English, double history and then double electives, the tuckshop had pizza pockets as the special, and the school prefects organised something for the whole school to do at lunchtime.

Tom had never been at a school where the student leadership had been so visible and direct in making the school a better place. Manny had explained to him early on that this was different, and it was a cultural thing that had begun years ago by a principal who was clearly well ahead of his time. Some weeks they just played music in the quad and encouraged people to submit their own mixed tapes, sometimes they had fundraisers that involved a huge amount of baked goods and sugar, while there were often educational sessions. Tom's favourite had been the staff vs student debate highlighted by Shep dropping his pants in front of the whole school to make a point that no-one could now recollect—all they could remember were his oversized Simpsons boxers and white legs.

However, this Tuesday had seemed to drag on forever—Tom couldn't remember looking at his watch so often, and despite the efforts of his teachers to keep him interested, all he could think about was going to training. It would be the first time that the team had been together since the game on Saturday, and Tom hoped that all of them being in the one place might remove the tension he was starting to feel. This hadn't been made any better by the prefect's decision to make the Tuesday lunchtime a mini rally to fire everyone up about the Grand Final. All the players had been invited onto an impromptu stage where they were given three cheers and a round of applause, and the captain was asked a couple of questions that he had responded to with clichés worthy of the occasion. It was noted that Albert had not been on the stage, but it was laughed away by the captain as being "one of those things that guys like him do," which had made Tom cringe, but the rest of the crowd had laughed at.

There was always time for him to go home after school, eat, get changed and wind down, but today he was not as calm. Even in the lead-up to last week's final he had not been too bothered about anything, just thinking about the enjoyment he got on Tuesdays and Thursdays, but today he just wanted to get to the ground, put his gear on and play. He was sure that if he could feel the thrill of the grass under his feet and the way his boots bit into the turf when he ran and kicked, then the reality he so enjoyed would come back, and the rest of the team would help him to realise that what he was nervous about was not really an issue.

He got home, dropped his school bag by the front door, called out absently to his mother, and expectedly got no response. He rummaged in the bottom of his cupboard for his boots, then snatched up his training top, shorts and socks, shoving them in his sports bag. Four Weetbix and three pieces of toast later, he was sitting by the kitchen bench, watching the clock, hoping that it would move faster. After 15 minutes of reading the paper, fiddling with his laces, looking in the cupboard for something else to eat and an attempt to touch his toes, he decided he was better off heading to Anzac Park, to see if there was anyone there he could talk to.

The park was either a five-minute bike ride or twenty-minute walk from his house. He decided to walk, hoping that the extra time it took would help him either clear his head or at least waste some time and help to ease his nerves. He locked his front door and slipped his key under the lone pot plant on the porch, then turned left and walked down his street.

As he walked, he kept looking for someone to make contact with, someone to say hello to, but the streets were strangely empty. It was only when he got within a few hundred metres of the club that he started to recognise people. They weren't teammates or coaches—they were the people who worked at the club full time or were the groundsmen, and his conversations with them had been limited throughout the year at best. As he turned through the gates of the oval, Bruce, the chief groundsman, who had been spot weeding around the edge of the oval, looked up at him and waved. "Wally!" Tom had to turn and look around, to make sure he was being spoken to—he'd never been a Wally despite his surname being Wallace, and the abbreviation of his name was a bit of a surprise. "How are ya?"

"Um, hi, Bruce. Good, I guess. Arm's a bit sore, but nothing too bad."

"You ready to smash 'em?"

"Smash who?"

"Masterton, ya dickhead. Masterton. They're your opponent, aren't they? This week?"

"Oh, right. Yep. Masterton. Going to smash them."

"Great, great. Town needs a win, no doubt. You know we haven't won anything since—"

"1975. Yeah, I know. Seventeen years ago. People keep telling me about how long it's been."

"Yep, 1975. Did you know I played that year? Hurt my leg midway through the season so couldn't play me best, but still helped."

"Really? I didn't know that. You played in that Grand Final?"

"No, played in the twos. Helped out though. We all did. Whole team effort that year. Even the kids played their role." He paused, lost in the memories of what might have been the greatest year he could remember. "Anyway, now it's your turn. Good luck!"

He turned away from Tom and restarted his spraying. Tom watched him for a second, and started to turn away, when Bruce barked at him without looking, "Don't miss your chance, Wally! Might only come once. Make sure the rest of them boys get that too. The 1975 team never played together again, and I haven't seen most of them for ten years!" Tom was lost for words, given the intensity of the voice, and before he could think of anything to respond with, Bruce had picked up his tools and wheelbarrow and moved further away. The moment was gone.

Tom jumped the fence and went on to the ground, walking along the boundary line, until he reached the gate that led to the grandstand and the change rooms. Instead of changing, he decided to sit in the stand and wait for his teammates to arrive. In Tom's mind, because neither of the senior teams had made the Grand Final, the juniors would be the only ones who would train, so the ground would not be as busy as usual, with only the team, the coaches and a handful of parents there. To his disbelief, at a quarter to five, half an hour before training started, a steady stream of people started to arrive, and take up their places around the ground.

Tom had no idea what was happening, until another one of his teammates, Jackson Fisher, or just Jacko, saw him in the stands and sat next to him. They had struck up an easy but superficial friendship over the year, with Tom enjoying Jacko's ability to work metaphors and swearing into every possible conversation. "Zoo today, mate, a fucking zoo. Look at these people. Haven't they got anything better to do?"

"But what are they doing here? There's no function, and there's nothing going on but us training."

"Fark! Don't you get it? They're here to watch us train!"

"Watch us train? Are you kidding?" The idea seemed ridiculous.

"Shit, no. It's for real. Fitz told me dad that he reckoned there'd be a couple of hundred of the vultures, just feeding on us for their own fun. Dickheads. Don't fuck it up tonight, mate, there'll be people everywhere. Let's go and get changed, eh, before we get mobbed."

The two stood up and made their way down the stairs and under the stand to the change rooms where they found a smattering of teammates, all in different states of preparation. Fitz was sitting in a corner with a clipboard on his lap. He had a biro dangling from his mouth, and was unconsciously using his lips to make the pen go up and down incessantly. None of the boys spoke to him, knowing that he was deeply involved in some overwrought piece of preparation. Tom glanced around for Albert and the other Aboriginal kids, but none had arrived—this wasn't unheard of, but even so, Tom's gut tightened. He hadn't thought about what might have happened if they didn't turn up and train, nor what would happen if they made a scene. He had imagined a lot of different scenarios for how the night might pan out, but the idea of them just absenting themselves to send a message wasn't one of them.

Training was meant to start at 5.15. By 5.10, almost all of the boys had arrived, and were ready to go. The crowd noise from outside was now more than a murmur, and the smell of sausages being cooked was making its way through to the boy's noses, and worse still, their stomachs. Fitz, who had been looking around expectantly, and hoping that the boys who hadn't arrived yet soon would, stood up and cleared his throat. "Right!" he barked, eyes scanning the room. "A couple of things. First, training is as normal as—"

With this, the door to the change room opened, and Albert poked his head around, smiling. "Hey, bruddas! Don't start without us!" With that, the five boys walked into the room, already changed and ready to train. They sat down, but this time they were spread around the room, not together. Tom wasn't sure how many of the others had noticed, but he did, and he sensed that something would happen. He was right.

Fitz looked at them all with a raised eyebrow from where he was still standing, then spoke. "As I was saying, training will still be as normal—we've said all year that the way we train will always show the way we play, and it's exactly the same tonight."

Fitz's remarks were met with a snort from Albert—when everyone looked at him, he smiled, and turned his palms upward. "What?" he asked. "Oh, right. The pre-training speech. Sorry, Fitz. Continue, please."

Fitz's voice rang out again, but with a small waver—his normally settled and calm demeanour had disappeared, but he went on. "You might notice a few more people out there than normal, but I want you to put that out of your heads, and just focus on the drills.

The rest is—"

Albert yawned. Not a small, hidden-behind-the-hand, 'I was up late' yawn, but a real, jaw-dislocating effort that again showed his theatrical ability. Fitz stopped, and his face showed red blotches as he tried to control his anger. "Anything bothering you, Albert?"

"What, me? No, Fitz. I mean, sorry to be rude, but we've all heard it. We know what we need to do and how training runs, and just how important it is. You've told us over and over."

"Sometimes, Albert, it's the basics that need to be stated. We've got a hu—"

"A huge game this week and we want to do our best for the team, the club and the town of Duneldin, and we owe it to ourselves to be the best we can be. Is that what you were going to say?"

"Well. Not exactly. I just wanted to remind—"

"Remind the boys of the things we set out at the start of the year and make sure we stay true to ourselves and the jumper we wear with pride. That too?"

"Well, I mean—" The rest of the boys were hanging on the edge of each sentence, unsure where it would go. They all loved Fitz, and would do whatever he asked of them, but this challenge to his authority appealed to their sense of drama. Fitz tried to change course. "Perhaps you'd like to say something, Albert. We know you're never short a word or two."

Albert smiled, and victory flashed through his eyes. He looked around the room, making sure he had the focus of the other four boys he had entered with. "Love to. How's this?" He stood up, and without a word, the other four stood with him.

Albert looked straight ahead, unwavering, and said, "We must forever conduct our struggle on the high plane of dignity and discipline. We must not allow our creative protests to degenerate into physical violence. Again and again we must rise to the majestic heights of meeting physical force with soul force."

He sat down, and as he did, Lachie, the tallest of the group, stood, following on from Albert seamlessly. "The marvellous new m-militancy which has engulfed our community must not lead us to distrust all white people, for many of our white brothers, as evidenced by their presence here today, have come to realise that their destiny is tied up with our destiny."

Benny, who had hardly spoken to the entire team for the whole year, then rose, and some boys heard his voice for the first time. "They have come to realise that their freedom is inextricably bound to our freedom. We cannot walk alone." He struggled with 'inextricably', but was still clear.

Steven Beats followed. "And as we walk we must make the pledge that we shall always march ahead. We cannot turn back."

Finally, Andy Phillips stood, and was the first to look around the room and at the whole of the team as he spoke. "There are those who are asking the devotees of civil rights, *'When will you be satisfied?'* We can never be satisfied."

The five then, in unison and looking straight ahead, finished by saying, "No, no, we are not satisfied, and we will not be satisfied until justice rolls down like waters and righteousness like a mighty stream."

A silence filled the room once they had finished speaking, and the five were motionless until they sat down in their places as one. The tension was broken unexpectedly.

"Mate, what the hell are you on about?" Mitch sat up, leaning forward, looking at Albert. "Try talking normally. No-one here understands a word you're saying."

Albert looked at him, trying not to laugh. "Oh, don't be too sure about that, skip."

"No, we really don't." Mitch looked at the rest of the team, and then back to Albert. "We just want to go out and train, not listen to you speak some weird crap that means nuthin'."

"Right. Means nothing. Were you listening?"

"I'm right here. We're all right here. What else could we do but listen?"

"You could have a think about what we were saying, and how it might relate to something going on out there." He gestured over his shoulder with a thumb. "You could do that."

Mitch paused, unsure of what he was being told. "Albert, no-one gives a shit about what you're going on about. All we want to do is go out there, run around, kick the footy and go home. Would it be okay to do that without you making it all about you?"

Albert laughed. "Okay, skip. Okay. It's about me." Albert sat down heavily, the sound of him landing reverberating through the room. He looked at the other four boys and smiled again. "We tried, lads, didn't we? Hey, Fitz. Should we go and give them what they want?"

Fitz's voice rang out, but it was flat and low. "Sure, boys. Let's go out there and train the house down. Enjoy yourselves!" The team all stood, and slowly made their way out of the sheds to the applause of the crowd. Tom waited until last, and looked at the area where Albert had stood, waiting for the lump that appeared in the back of his throat to get to a size he hoped no-one could see.

When training had finished, the boys made their way to the same part of the boundary where they ran on and received another round of applause from the crowd. Tom couldn't believe what he was hearing—it was as if they had just won a game mid-season.

They all sat in a group and started their warm downs, and as they did, he made sure he was near Albert. Tom sat down and made to stretch his groins and hamstrings, looking at Albert as he did.

"Mate, that was crazy," he said.

"Whaddaya mean?"

"Your little presentation at the start of training. I mean, good performances and everything, but what was the point?"

"If you don't know, then there's not much point explaining it to you."

Tom thought for a second, then looked at him again. "So, is that it?"

"Again, whaddaya mean?"

"I mean, is that your protest? You borrow a brilliant speech and you humiliate the coach and captain. Is there more or is that it?"

"Ha! At least someone got the speech. Well played. What do I have to protest against?"

"Jesus, Albert, you know what I'm talking about."

"No, I don't, because I don't think you know what you're talking about. Protest? Humiliation? Why would I do that? To bring about change? I don't think so. Not much point in a place like this. Let's talk about something else, something that will be easy for you to talk about."

"Like what?"

"Like footy. Ever notice how fair and even it is? How when you step over the line everyone's meant to be the same, and that the same rules apply to everyone?"

"Ye-es, I guess so. Why?" Tom felt like the conversation had moved onto shaky ground, and that he had no control over where it was going.

"Well, have you thought about the way the team is selected?

Where everyone plays? Who the captain is? It doesn't just happen."

"Mate, it's just Fitz. He does it all. Who else would be involved?"

"Look around you. Look at the machine we're a part of. Nothing happens here without other people knowing what's going on. Fitz makes some of the decisions, but he doesn't make all of them. Is Mitch really the best player? Does Lachie deserve to start on the bench every week? Why doesn't Benny ever win a coach's award, when everyone else has about ten? You got one and hardly touched the ball."

Again, Tom's mind started to do cartwheels, and he couldn't stop them. All the things Albert said were true, but at the same time, there was something in his mind that stopped him from fully accepting what he was being told. He wanted to respond, but the words wouldn't form in his mouth. "You know what?" Albert asked. "Forget it. It's not about you, it's about all this. This week is supposed to be some kind of celebration, but who for? Who is actually going to be celebrating if we win?"

"What do you mean? We all will be. You, me, the whole team, Fitz, and apparently the whole town."

"Yep. The whole town. But sometimes, the whole town doesn't mean everybody, does it? Come to my part of town and see who's celebrating Saturday night." Tom sighed, deflated. He knew what Albert meant and couldn't argue against it. He looked at the rest of the team, and the joy on his teammates' faces, then back at Albert, and the scorn on his. Then he looked at Fitz, and Frank, the president, who had walked over and was slapping the coach on the back, sharing a joke. Even though he was amongst almost a hundred people, Tom felt alone.

For the second time in as many visits to the ground, Tom left, mind racing. He knew that everything Albert had said was right, but also that it was becoming skewed, affected by his anger. He made his way to the gate, dragging his feet, and wishing he had brought his bike after all. The walk home seemed like it was going to take a lot longer than twenty minutes, and he just wanted to be at home, in his room, doing anything but thinking about football. As he got to the kerb side, a white van pulled up, with its window wound down. Tom recoiled, thinking it would be another well-wisher, ready to give his advice, but a familiar voice spoke to him.

"Mate, what are you doing?" Fitz's familiar baritone drawled out of the car window.

"Oh, hi, Fitz. How's it going?"

"Good, good. Are you walking home?"

"Yep." He felt like he should say something else, but was unsure what.

"Hop in. I'll drop you off."

"You sure? It's not out of your way?"

"Tom, the town is about 6 km wide. Nothing's out of the way. I wanted to talk to you about something anyway."

"Okay. Thanks." Tom opened the door, and looked at the front seat, which was covered with papers, a footy jumper and Fitz's prized clipboard. Fitz looked at the seat and started laughing. "Obviously, footy takes over everything at this time of the year. Just throw that shit—sorry, throw that crap over the back." Tom did as he was told, then climbed in, and put on his seat belt, noticing at the same time Fitz wasn't wearing his. "You did well tonight," Fitz said. "Thought you trained like a champ."

"Oh, thanks. Didn't seem that different than normal, but it was fun. Good to get out and run around. How are you feeling?"

"Me? Great! Couldn't be better. Bring on Saturday! Best day of the year and I can't wait to show the town what we're capable of."

"Right. Yep. Are you nervous?"

"Nervous? Are you kidding? What have I got to be nervous about? We've been the best team all year and we'll keep being the best team until 11 o'clock Saturday morning."

"Right." Tom had no idea how to counter Fitz's unbridled enthusiasm, so he didn't say anything. There was a short lull in the conversation and without really thinking, Tom blurted out, "What did you think of Albert's stunt?"

"Stunt?" Fitz seemed to not know what Tom was talking about.

"Yeah, at the start of training, with him and the other Aboriginal boys."

"Not much. Got the feeling that everyone's a bit nervous and that they have different ways of dealing with it. I'd say it's as weird to walk to training, get there 45 minutes early and then walk home when you could easily ride a bike or get a lift. Everyone's different."

Tom half smiled at the ribbing. "Yeah, but—"

"Look, I've known those boys for years. Saw them first when they turned up to the club as eight-year-olds and could hardly kick. Now they're almost men and getting ready to play seniors. Albert could go all the way and get drafted to the VFL."

"You mean AFL."

"Whatever. Still the VFL in my book. Anyway, he's always pushed, always. It's what makes him so good. Can't be as good as that and stay within the rules. As long as he plays as well as he can on Saturday, then I don't care if he turns up to training in a clown suit and turns cartwheels instead of running laps. Sometimes you gotta let the great ones just be different. Look at Gary Ablett." Fitz stopped speaking, as if the mention of Ablett was enough to stop the conversation. "Now look, I wanted to talk to you about something, about your game. On Saturday, I want you to—"

Tom sensed that his moment to tell Fitz what he knew was slipping. "Fitz, I have to tell you something. It's not right here. With Albert. He's not right. Something happened to him on Saturday, and he's really angry."

"Whaddya mean? What happened?"

"Someone told him he couldn't play with their kids because he's Aboriginal, and it set him off."

"Who told him that?"

"Some woman who was at the game. I don't know her. Mrs Thorpe, I think."

"Thorpey! Ha! Was she drunk when she said it?"

"Yes, I think so."

"Course she was. She's always pissed at the footy, and she thinks she knows everything. Has a great time yelling at me telling me how to coach, too." Fitz's car had turned into Tom's street, but he didn't want the conversation to end. "Look, tell Albert not to worry about her. She's a dickhead, her family are dickheads, and they always will be. They've had a chip on their shoulder about something ever since they moved here. She's not the town, and she never will be."

"Why isn't he captain?"

"What? Who?"

"Albert. If he's so good, why isn't he the captain?" The words were rolling out of Tom now, and he couldn't stop them. "Mitch can play all right, but he's not the best player. It should be Albert."

Fitz paused, and seemed to be carefully choosing his words, and a look appeared on his face Tom couldn't place. "We have talked about it. The club, I mean. But think about it. Should the captain be disrespectful to the coach? To the rest of the team?

Pull stunts? Make a dick of himself and others? No. Albert's been doing this stuff for years. He'd never be captain because he won't play the whole game."

The car pulled up outside Tom's house, and the front light called to him. "Right. Okay. Thanks. Thanks. Here we are then. Thanks for the lift, Fitz. See you."

"Hang on, Tom. I need to tell you something. On Saturday, I'm giving you a job, a big job. You know their number 9?"

Tom was jolted out of his thinking about Albert.

"Yeah?"

"I want you to tag him. Run with him the whole day. Don't let him get a kick. Squeeze him like a massive pimple, and drive him nuts. If we can stop him then we've got the game in the bag. You up for it?"

"What?"

"Number 9. He's their best player and I want you to stop him."

"Me? Really? I've never done anything like that. Are you sure I'm the right guy for it?"

"Yep. Wouldn't ask you otherwise. Now I know you don't normally do these kinds of jobs, but I want you to do it 'cos you're smart, and you're a thinker. You get what I'm asking you to do. Some of the other boys will want to be heroes, and I'll need some of them to do other things."

"What about Burkey? Or Benny? They're smart players, and they can run all day."

"Nup. They can't do it. Not like you can. And I've got other things for them to do. It's your job. Okay? Okay."

"Okay then. Thanks. I guess." Tom started to open the door, and as he did Fitz thrust out his hand. Tom shook it and smiled. "Thanks for the lift, Fitz."

"Anytime."

Tom shut the car door and Fitz revved the engine, again heaving away from the kerb. Tom said "Bloody hell!" to the street light and went inside.

He opened the front door and went into the kitchen, where he found a note from his mum, scrawled in a way that told him she had written it quickly. "Dinner in fridge. Turn on oven to 190, warm for 20 minutes. I'll be late. Won't see you. Do your homework and read a book. Love."

He went to the fridge and opened it, where he saw half a chicken-and-vegetable pie on a plate, with a cut up tomato and cucumber next to it. He did as he was told—taking the salad off the plate just in time—and half an hour later had eaten a lukewarm dinner that had filled him but still left him feeling empty. He thought about homework, then discarded the thought, knowing that his mind wouldn't really be focused on it, and that he would only spend the night thinking about football, which sadly was the last thing he wanted to focus on. He thought about writing a letter to some of his friends back in the city, then gave up on that too, knowing that he wouldn't really be able to tell them what was going on anyway. Eventually he settled on a book about a fireman who burned things instead of putting them out that his mum had been recommending for years, and he fell asleep with the book on his chest, still in his clothes.

When Jenny came in and found him, took off his shoes and rolled him into bed, she couldn't have possibly known about the confusion of his dreams, and of how they involved escape and running, but always with the feeling of being chased.

CHAPTER 05

WEDNESDAY

Tom's timetable was written out and stuck on the fridge, and one of his morning jobs was to look at it, and make sure that he had everything he needed for the day. He saw that his last two periods were geography and biology, the subjects he liked the least. He had questioned the relevance of them but chose them anyway. He knew that when the time came at the end of year 11, he would drop one of them, to focus on his strengths, history and English. Regardless, he packed his bag and quickly made lunch, grabbing everything he needed to make a ham and cheese sandwich and crushing the ingredients together in almost record time before he left the house, locking the door behind him. His mum had left the house early that morning—he had briefly seen her on the way out, and she promised she would take him out to the pub for a meal that night to make up for her recent work-related absences, and to give him the chance to tell her what was going on in his world. She made some fleeting mention of council meetings as a reason for her absence, which always amused Tom, given the seeming invisibility of the work that the council was doing.

He grabbed his bike and helmet, and started to ride down the driveway, but just as he did, he looked up and noticed Manny standing at the top of his driveway. He did a double take—

the idea of her just being in the neighbourhood was odd, given she lived a few streets closer to the school than he did, and that she'd have to go backward to get to his house. They hardly ever travelled to school together anyway, given the difference in their mornings—she was an early riser who liked to get to school early and watch the buildings "wake up", as she put it, whereas he tried to get there right on time, maximising the amount of time he had at home before he left.

"Hey," he said.

"Hey, yourself. Want to head to school together?"

"Sure. Of course." His mind ticked over quickly. "What would you do if I said no?"

"Awkwardly walk on the other side of the street to you and spend the rest of my days forgetting that this ever happened. Why would you say no?"

"To see you awkwardly walk on the other side of the street and …" He trailed off, with a smile in his eyes, and she laughed at him.

"No, you wouldn't. You're not that kind of a turd. I mean, you're a turd, just not that kind."

"Thanks. I think." He looked at her. "So, what's going on?"

"You mean why am I here?"

"Yep, basically."

"I don't know. Call it sympathy. I just wanted to find out how you were going and if you'd talked to Albert."

"Albert? I tried. He basically told me to go away and to not get involved. Something's going on though. He and the rest of his crew turned up to training last night and for five minutes he humiliated the coach and gave a sermon on equality. It was brutal."

"What did they do? The club, I mean."

"Nothing. Fitz kind of laughed it off and put it down to nerves and boys being boys. The rest of the team thought he was just being a dickhead.”

“What did you think?”

“I think it’s only a start. I tried to talk to him afterwards, and he pointed out a few other things about the club, and they kind of reflected what you said yesterday. It’s shit. I’m wishing I’d never decided to play.”

“You don’t mean that.”

“I do and I don’t. I mean, I loved being involved and taking what being part of the team did for me as someone who was new to the town, but now that this is all happening, and this week too! Fitz gave me a massive job on Saturday, and I should be thinking about that, but I’m not.”

“What was the job?”

“He wants me to play on their best player and make his life hell. I’m not sure exactly how to do that, but if I do it right, then I think we’re a chance.”

“Hmm. Stop their best player and you might win. High-quality tactics there, Tom. Do you reckon he came up with that himself, or got it from a book?” She had a serious look on her face, but the raised eyebrow gave her sarcasm away.

“Very funny. It’s a big job. An important one. I don’t know if I can do it.”

“You’ll be fine. And as for Albert starting something, what can he do? It’s a team sport. Even if he tries to poison the half time oranges or puts Dencorub in your undies, it’s still a team game. There’s everyone else, and everyone else wants to win.”

“Yeah, maybe. Can we talk about something else? I know you came to talk to me about Albert and footy, but isn’t there anything else?”

"Sure. My sister sent me a new tape she recorded from the radio. Listen to this—it's got R.E.M. on one side and someone called Tori Amos on the other. She's gorgeous and angsty. You'll love it." She took her headphones from around her neck and gave them to him. When they were on his ears, she pressed play on her Walkman and for a few minutes Tom got to escape into the music and away from his own thoughts.

There seemed to be a lull in the Grand Final discussion amongst the students, for no obvious reason. Perhaps it was because there was nothing new to say—training wasn't on again until tomorrow, and there were only so many answers that even the boys could give about how they thought they'd go. There was a bit of talk about how people were getting to the game—even though Duneldin had finished on top of the ladder the game was going to be played at the largest ground in the area, in Horminton, about 45 minutes' drive away. They were also the first of three Grand Finals on the day, with the reserves and the seniors being played afterward. Most people planned on staying for the other two games, as there was always a carnival atmosphere that symbolised the end of the season, and the league were well organised in the kind of entertainment they put on for families. Tom enjoyed not being questioned or hassled by everyone in the school, and for the first four periods of the day, he managed to almost enjoy what was going on around him.

At lunchtime he took his now squashed and almost edible sandwiches out of his bag and headed to the quadrangle, where he was surprised to see Albert sitting amongst a collection of students. For the week so far he hadn't been seen much, and Tom had assumed he had been in the library or hiding from the crowds who were keen to talk to him about the game. The throng around him was thick, so

Tom decided to sit away from him with the hope of catching him sometime during the forty-five minutes they had as a break. He didn't really know what he'd say, but at least he had something to talk about, given the role Fitz had assigned him last night. Before too long, Albert had seen Tom, and was making his way over to him, smiling. Tom, wary of what might be behind the smile, looked at Albert, only nodding his greeting. Albert sat on the concrete ledge next to Tom.

"Brudda."

"Brudda. How you going?" Tom didn't often use the term to address Albert but was doing everything to keep the conversation on a lighthearted level.

"Good. Great. Loving every day at Duneldin High. You?"

"The same. Looking forward to geo with Roberts and biology with Ruddick this afternoon."

"Oh yeah, bio. Let's hope we get to cut something open, not just take notes off the blackboard." They both laughed, and there was a pause in the conversation Tom filled quickly.

"Hey, can I tell you something?"

"Sure. Is it interesting?"

"Don't know. It's about footy, and about Saturday."

"Shit, really? I'm sick of talking about it."

"I know, I know, me too. But I got a lift home from Fitz last night, and he's given me a job. In the game."

"Really? What job? Waterboy? Orange squeezer? The guy that gives massages when we come off the ground?"

"No, he wants me to run with their number 9. The best player. Told me it was my job to make sure he doesn't get a kick. Or something like that."

"Right. Did he have any other jobs for anyone?"

"Not that he told me about. Just said he had a few things planned, but that was it for me."

"Right. Big job. Did he actually tell you how to stop him?"

"Well, no. I mean, I guess that's coming on Thursday."

Albert paused, looked around and sighed. "Have you ever seen Fitz miss a game?"

Tom blinked. "One of ours? Of course not. He's the coach."

"Do you reckon we have people who travel around to watch the opposition?"

"Um, well, now you mention it ..."

"Of course not. The seniors do, but we're just the under 18s. So what special instructions do you think he's going to give you except run next to him and tackle him when he gets it? He wants you to do a job, but it's like telling a kid to be a carpenter and hoping they know how to use a hammer. There needs to be a bit more, right?"

"Well, yeah. What would you do if you were me?"

"I'd get totally used to looking at his left ear, left shoulder and left butt cheek."

"Why? Is that his best side or something?"

"No, dickhead. Number 9 is left-footed. If you stay on his right and he steps away from you, he's on his left side and he gets a kick away when he gets it, and you know he's gonna get it. If you're on his left then he has to move right and maybe have to kick right-footed, and he hasn't got a right foot. Hardly any left-footers do, they all run on to their left. Even Michael Long, and he's a genius. You won't always be able to stop him, but you can maybe stop what he does when he gets it."

Tom was shaking his head. The logic of the argument was impressive. He turned to look at Albert, and found he was now standing. Tom looked up.

"Thanks. I mean, really. That's so smart."

Albert smiled. "Nah, mate, it's just knowing the game, and knowing how people play it." He turned to walk away, but then looked back. "Maybe you should go and ask Mitch how to play him. See what he says." Tom knew it was a challenge, but not one he was all that keen on taking up.

Geography hadn't been as bad as Tom had expected—in fact, he walked out with the bemused look of a boy who had learnt something in spite of his greatest wishes. He thanked Mrs Roberts for the lesson, and walked to biology with weather maps and synoptic charts swimming in his brain. The lesson had dealt with the emergence of storm cells and intense weather patterns, and Tom now felt that when he watched the news at night, he'd have a bit more of an idea what the weather man was trying to tell him.

He made his way through the corridors to the science block, and found his teacher directing traffic. Ms Ruddick was standing outside the room they were meant to be in, waving her arms, shuffling the students to a new location, away from the lab and into one of the school's three demountables. The students were groaning—not just because of the extra distance they had to travel, but because it meant they wouldn't be doing anything practical today. The labs were where the interesting stuff happened, and the classrooms where textbooks and photocopies awaited.

Tom didn't really want to admit it, but he had always had a minor crush on his biology teacher. Yes, she was tall, and yes she was blonde, but in his mind that wasn't it. Tom's first day of school had been a blur and had ended with biology. His mind was filled with timetables and expectations and apprehension, and after the bell had rung to dismiss the students, he had sat quietly in the back of the room, staring at the blackboard as if he couldn't work out what was written there. His teacher, Ms Ruddick, stood at the front of the classroom on the raised platform she had been teaching from, and was shuffling papers, which cracked Tom's reverie. She didn't notice Tom still sitting in the back row, and he didn't let on that he was watching her. Just as Tom was about to stand up and leave, she let out a long "Fuuuuuuuuuck … me." He snorted when he heard her swear, and she looked up. "Oh, shit! I didn't—" She paused. "Apologising for swearing by swearing. Pretty classy. I didn't know you were there."

"No, I guessed not. I didn't notice you dropping the f-bomb when you were talking about coursework and exams, so I kinda figured you thought we were all gone. Do you always swear like that at the end of a lesson?"

She looked at him and laughed. "I do actually. I used to do it out of frustration, but now it's just a bit of a habit. It's like letting the day go." She paused. "Sorry, who are you?"

"Tom. Tom Wallace. It's my first day."

"Oh, of course. Ha! I can imagine you going home and your mum asking what you learned today and you saying that your bio teacher swore like a truck driver. How was it?"

"How was what?"

"Your first day. Duneldin High School."

She had packed her bag and started to move to the door. With a shoulder she indicated to him that she was going out the door and that he should move with her. He quickly stood up and moved out into the hallway. "Good, I guess. Nothing bad happened, I didn't embarrass myself and I feel okay about coming back tomorrow. It was weird, it was as if no-one knew that I was here."

"Oh, they noticed, but it will take them a while to say anything.

So many kids come and go because of their parents' jobs that new students aren't that foreign. It was weird this year though—you're the only newbie. They'll warm up soon. Do you know where you're going?"

It was a question his mother had been asking him in a different context over the summer, and he gave the response without thinking. "Does anyone?"

"You're quick. Sorry, Voltaire. I meant, do you know how to get out of the school?"

"Oh, yeah, thanks. My buddy this morning was very thorough."

"Great. See you next lesson. And if you do tell anyone about what happened, please, you know, kind of …"

"Oh, no worries. It was funny. Thanks, miss." She strode off, and from then on, Tom always looked forward to the lessons, imagining the swearing in her internal monologue at the same time she was trying to teach them the subject.

When they were all seated and settled, Ms Ruddick wrote a single word on the board—GENETICS. She turned to them and said plainly. "Right. I know you were all looking forward to doing some lab work today, but the year 12 chemistry kids have a major assessment coming up, and they need to use them for their work. So, here we are. Before you start complaining, I'm sure you'll want the same thing next year when you're all doing biology." With this she smiled at them, pointing a finger, and scanned the room. "And you will all do biology, otherwise I'll find you and hurt you, okay? Anyway, today we're starting a new topic. What's the word on the board? Lily?"

Lily, who had been picking at her nails and apparently not paying any attention, looked up and said. "Um, genetics, miss."

"Good, Lily. What's genetics?"

"No idea, miss. Something to do with biology."

"Very clever. Ella?"

"Yes, miss?"

"What's genetics? Why would I write it on the board in such big letters?"

"'Cos you have to, miss? It said on the planner we're doing it, so you need to write it."

"Very clever, Ella, but what are genetics? Why would we study them?"

"Don't know."

"Okay. Anyone want to help Lily and Ella out? What are genetics?"

There was silence throughout the room. Even though the kids in this class were a little bit above average in terms of their scientific knowledge, no-one dared suggest an answer, worried that they might be seen as being wrong, or even worse from a social sense, right.

Ms Ruddick sighed. "All right then. Genetics are a part of us— they're what make us what we are. Our genes are part of a code we all carry around that help to make us completely unique—no two people are exactly alike, and one of the reasons for that is the code that creates us is like no other. It's like the information in us that gets passed down through families—parents from grandparents, grandparents from great-grandparents, great-grandparents back and so on. We get particular characteristics from our parents, and they got them from their parents—what you are is a representation of the weirdness of genetics, and the complete randomness that comes from reproduction."

From the side of the room, Mitch called out, "Is that why Genevieve's a ranga?"

"Sorry, Mitch?"

"Is that why Genevieve's a ranga? A redhead. Is that because of genetics?" Genevieve, sitting on the other side of the room, blushed, having been dragged into a discussion she wanted no part of.

"Actually, yes, it is. There's a genetic combination in everyone that gives them hair colour, eye colour."

"And is that why Martin looks like one of those Albanian kids?" Martin too looked at Mitch for half a second, then down at his desk.

"You mean an albino?"

From behind Tom, he heard Albert snort appreciation at Ms Ruddick's takedown.

Mitch went on as if he hadn't noticed. "Whatever. Yeah, is that why he's so pale?"

"Again, yes it is."

"And would that be why some people run slower than others? Tom, say, isn't as fast as me or has reflexes as good. Is that genes?" Tom smiled, ready to laugh—it was widely known he wasn't super quick, and being the butt of a joke only amused him.

Like a bullwhip, Albert's voice cracked across the class. "Might be, but it doesn't really explain you being a complete dickhead though, does it? I mean, some things can't be genetic, they have to be learned, and—"

"Albert! Cut it out!" Mitch was ready to take up the challenge, but Ms Ruddick's voice crushed the beginning of his protest. "That's just not necessary. Stop it now."

"It's true though, isn't it?" Albert sat up and leant forward. "Genetically, we're all pretty similar, right? We all supposedly evolved from the same spot, and when you think about how long humans have been alive, there hasn't really been much of a chance for us to be that different. Heaps of species of dogs and cats and other animals, but not a huge difference in humans."

"Yes, that's right. You're spot on."

"So it doesn't explain stupidity. Or other things. Like people thinking they're better than someone else because of their skin colour."

"No …"

"Then what does? What explains the belief that one species is superior to another if you can't put it down to genetics?"

"I'm sorry, Albert. If I had an answer to that, I wouldn't be a science teacher at Duneldin High School."

Mitch had been following the conversation, his small eyes jumping from teacher to student and back. From nowhere, he blurted, "It's not genetics, mate. There are a bunch of other things that make us different. Parents, lifestyle, where you live, what you do with your spare time, heaps of stuff."

"Maybe, mate. But none of the things you're talking about make us genuinely different. You and I, we're pretty similar if you use those ideas. In fact, I reckon I've got you on a few of them. But there you are, thinking you're better."

"Who said I think I'm better?"

"Boys! Right! Leave it, now!" Ms Ruddick had raised her voice to a level the class hadn't heard before. "I don't want to hear it, and neither does anyone else. You want to debate it? Debate it in your own time, not mine. This is science, and we're going to deal in facts. Like scientists. Open your textbooks, and head to chapter 6. I want you to read the first eight pages, and then answer the Investigation questions on page 136. Got it? Good. Start work, and the first person who even breathes the wrong way is staying behind to help me clean the storeroom with a freaking toothbrush after school."

As one, the class exhaled, opened their textbooks and started work. Tom tried as hard as he could to concentrate on the pages in front of him, but he couldn't stop his eyes flicking across the classroom, trying to look at Mitch and Albert, somehow at the same time. Mitch had his head down and was chewing his pen, but continually nudged Nick, the boy next to him, and the two of them shared a joke Tom wished he didn't know about. Albert sat bolt upright, looking at the pages in front of him, reading intently. Tom knew that he was using what he was learning and turning it to his argument—he also knew that the fight wasn't over.

The lesson came to an end, and Ms Ruddick told them to pack up. Tom didn't feel like what had happened in the class earlier was finished, and it wasn't long until he was proven right. Mitch sat back in his chair, swinging on two legs.

"Miss, you coming to the footy Saturday?"

"What footy would that be then?"

"Oh come on, miss. The Grand Final!"

"Oh, that footy. Well, actually, no, I won't. I'm heading to Adelaide for a family birthday—I have to drive five hours to get there and five hours back, so I'll be leaving as soon as the bell rings on Friday."

"But don't you want to see us win? First time—"

"In 17 years. Yes, I know. It's all very exciting." Tom noticed the droll tone in her voice, and wondered where it came from.

"Hey, miss?" Albert's voice was coated with honey.

"Yes, Albert." She looked at him, warily.

"Do you think genetics will have anything to do with who wins on Saturday?"

"Why would it?"

"Oh, you know. It might affect how we play. Or how some of us play."

"Maybe. But genetics shouldn't affect things like practice and training though. That's not genetics, it's preparing properly—that's another type of science."

Mitch had resented the topic moving out of his control, and said, "Mate, the only thing genetics will do is affect how much we party when we win. Some of us will go home, some will go hard. It's about the species."

"Darwinism comes later, Mitch. And don't do anything stupid."

"Oh, I won't, I'll leave that to Albert and his boys. They're his genetics, right there." The smile on Mitch's face was absolute, as if he believed he had played a blindsiding checkmate.

Tom expected Albert to explode, but he was surprisingly calm. He took a deep breath, looked at Ms Ruddick, then said, smiling, "That's right, brudda. Me and the boys are gonna be living out our genetic dream. All over the field. You'll love it."

"What does that even mean?" Mitch tried to undercut Albert's tone, but couldn't.

"Ask me at 11 o'clock Saturday. Have a safe drive, Ms Ruddick." With that, Albert left the classroom, before the bell had even left. The rest of the class looked at him; they were amazed at the level of his confidence and the guts it took to leave without being dismissed. Before anyone could say anything, the bell rang, and the rest of the class filed out.

Tom was one of the last to go, and before he left the room, Ms Ruddick called to him. "Tom? A minute?"

"Sure." She waited until the classroom had cleared, and Tom said quickly, "I bet you'll want to swear your head off today, miss."

"Hell, yes. What was all that about? Are they okay?"

"Yes. No. I don't know. Albert is being so weird lately. I don't know what is happening with him."

"In all my time teaching genetics at this school, I've never seen anything like that. It usually takes kids a while to say or do something stupid, but it was as if he was ready for it and wanted a stink. And they're meant to be on the same team!"

"I know. It'll be all right. We'll win the game, and then hopefully all this kind of stupid tension will blow over."

"Do you think so?"

"Not sure. Hope so. It can't be good if it keeps going on. Albert will do something really dumb, and people won't forgive him."

"Maybe. Anyway, see you next lesson. I hope it goes well."

"Yes, miss. Me too."

He walked towards the school exit via his locker, only stopping long enough to get his bag and a book or two. Again, he was amazed at the way that the issue he had been trying to deal with had raised its head again, this time in a classroom.

He had been impressed with the way that Ms Ruddick had been able to shut the stupidity of the argument down, but the fact that it had come about in the first place was what shocked him. Was it really that obvious? Did people in the town really have this attitude sitting below the surface, covering it over when they saw fit? Tom had seen enough the year he had spent in Duneldin to know that the Aboriginal community was an important part of the fabric of the town, no more so than at the footy club. He had seen people—even people that he now thought less of—applauding and wondering at some of the skill that had been seen on the field, but now he wondered what they said when everyone's back was turned and doors were closed.

He knew that going after Albert and trying to talk to him was a waste of time, and he was also convinced that Albert had a plan for the weekend, but what could he do? The worst thing would be not to play, or make a scene of some sort—a protest? A banner? Wear the Indigenous flag onto the field? Tom couldn't think what Albert and the Aboriginal boys could do that would make them feel like they had succeeded. Tom knew that whatever it was they did, they couldn't possibly hope to change the mindset of the town. Albert might have some kind of pyrrhic victory but he wasn't going to win a war that the history of the town suggested he couldn't begin to fight.

Home was empty. His mother had promised dinner, but not what time she would be home to take him out, and it left him again sitting at home waiting for something to happen. He wandered out into the backyard and looked at the house—a small, double-fronted Federation bungalow with two halves of a house joined by the kitchen and family area at the back, and then the back door through the laundry. Tom had hated it when they first moved in, with its weatherboards and tin roof, but now he had started to see the charm, even if they did nothing to maintain it. He then looked at the limp state of the lawn and the edging around it. Between the two of them they had never really paid much attention to what was happening out here, and once a month Tom helped to earn his pocket money by running an old lawn mower over it. As for weeding, they never really saw the need, and there were no flowers to speak of—a couple of lonely shrubs inhabited the garden beds that lined the fence, but they seemed to survive more thanks to their own will to live than any help from anyone else.

Tom thought about the groundskeeper at Anzac Park, and how dedicated he was to keeping the ground looking so perfect, and decided that it was time for him to try to do the same thing. He got down on his hands and knees and started crawling around the concrete ledge that divided the grass from the garden, and pulled every weed he could out. The ones that wouldn't come he left, but he was surprised at just how easy it was for him to remove what had grown there. Some were large enough to be at eye level as he crawled around, and after half an hour, he found that he had done a reasonable job. He then went to the garage, switched on the light and found the lawn mower. He took it to the backyard, and primed the engine, then yanked on the starter cord. It failed to fire. He tried again, and after a short spluttering, it died. He opened the fuel tank and looked inside. With no sign of any petrol, he went back to the garage, and looked for the fuel can his mother had bought in January. He found it and picked it up—it was empty, and with that, his gardening desire escaped. He put the mower away, and then sat on the back step of the house, looking at nothing in particular.

The phone rang, dragging him away from his daydreams of a bigger city, a place where he could easily escape, and where he could walk down the street and no-one would know who he was. He jumped at the sound, and ran inside to where the phone was plugged in.

"Wallace house?"

"Tom, it's Mum. Are you ready for dinner?"

"Sure, but where are you?"

"I'm still at the office. Things are getting pretty hectic here, what with the footy and all the council stuff that's been happening. Should be okay though. Do you want to just meet me at the Commercial?"

"Can't you come and pick me up?"

"By the time I got out of here and back home then back here, you'd be here, so no, I can't. Are you going to ride or walk?"

"Ride, I think."

"You got your lights? It's almost dark."

"Yep. Got them. See you soon."

He had made it to the pub in reasonable time, and looked in the window to see his mother sitting at a table, reading a book. He knocked on the window and she looked up, saw him and waved. He went to the door, entered, and sat down with her. They talked loosely about what their day had been like, until she said directly, "I'm bloody starving. What do you want? I'm not waiting for them to come and take the order."

"Right. I'll just have the parma with chips, thanks."

"Good choice. I need iron, so I'm having the steak. Drink?"

"Coke."

"So, water then."

"Juice?"

"Oh, all right. I'm having a drink. God, how I need one."

Jenny came back to the table and sat down. She looked at him and saw the pain in him. "Tom, come on. What is it? Whatever it is, it can't be that bad."

"Mum, how long are we going to be here?"

"I beg your pardon?"

"Here. Duneldin. How long are we going to live here for?"

"Bloody hell, Tom. I just wanted to have a quiet dinner, then go home, read a book and go to sleep."

"Well, you can, but I'd love to know. How long do you see us staying here?"

"I don't know. A year. Six. I don't know. Why? What's happened? I thought you liked it. I know it's not the city, but even so, it's okay, isn't it?"

"It is. I mean, it was, but not at the moment."

"What's happened? Is it the footy mania? I know it's crazy at the moment, but regardless of what happens, the season will end on Saturday, and you won't have to think about it for months. You can go back to a bit of normality then, can't you?"

"Yes. No. I don't know. It's not about the footy. I mean, it's part of it, but it's … it's this Albert thing."

"You mean what you told me about on Sunday? That? I thought that would have blown over. He's got enough to think about with the game on Saturday, doesn't he?"

"But that's just it, Mum. The game on Saturday." Cookie, the pub's chef, had walked over to the table, and was stroking his ample stomach, right in front of them. Both Tom and his mum sat back instinctively, surprised by the intrusion and the size of his girth.

"How you two doin'?" Cookie's gravelly voice sounded worse than normal, as if he'd upped his daily dosage of cigarettes.

Jenny took the lead. "Yes, good, thanks, all great."

"What are yous havin'?" Cookie stank of grease and sweat, and Tom's nose started to send messages to his brain to retreat quickly. The chef leant over, making it obvious he was more interested in talking to Tom than to Jenny.

"I'm having a parma, and Mum's having the steak."

"Righto. How're ya feelin'?"

"Great! Great. Just talking with me mum."

"Are ya! Good one. But how're ya feelin'? Ya ready for the weekend?" He winked at Jenny, who looked on in disbelief.

"Um, yeah, I guess. Should be great."

"Yep, sure should be. Hmph." He seemed to have reached his

conversational limit and straightened up to go. "Have a good night then, and make sure you get enough sleep! You've got a big job Sat'day—stop that number 9 and we'll have some new silverware for the club, and ya photo can go up on the wall there." He gestured to the gallery of teams that had caught Tom's eye earlier in the year. You'll be there forever! Seeyas."

Tom looked at his mother and shook his head.

"Jesus. As if I'd want to be on the wall of this pub forever. And how does he know about this weekend? I told two people about the job I've got, and now everyone knows. You can't shit in this town without everyone being able to smell it."

"Yes. True. Interestingly put, but anyway. What were you saying about Albert and the game?"

"I don't know. He's got some big protest planned, I think—like some sort of political thing to make people think about what happened, and what's been happening."

"A protest—what, like a sit-in?"

"Yeah, maybe. Or not turning up, or, or something else. I dunno."

"Albert is a lot of things, but he's not dumb. He won't do anything too crazy, because he knows he has to front up to the rest of his life on Monday, and he knows his family will be targeted if he goes over the top. Whatever he has planned, it's not going to change anything anyway. This town is what it is."

"I know, and that brings me back to my point. How long do we have to stay here? This place, Mum, it isn't us."

"Maybe not, but for the time being it has to be. Tom, you're 16, almost 17. You're in year 11. In a year and a bit's time, you'll be finished school, and I absolutely will support you doing whatever it is you like. Uni, job, whatever. And I know you won't be able to do it here, and I'll support you moving. But I'll be staying here for at least a couple more years, at least. We can't just up and leave. I've only just started at the paper, and if I was to quit, I don't know where we'd go. No-one else would offer me this kind of job, and I need to do something. I'm trying to be a good journo, and it's hard out here, but once I get a bit more settled and a few more people get to know me, then maybe I can head somewhere else. You'll probably be in a capital city, and I'll come and visit you as often as I can."

Their food arrived, and they ate quickly, with hardly a word. When they finished, they both stood, and as they made for the door, Jenny hooked her arm inside her son's.

"I get that you're stressed out about this 'cos you think it isn't right, and it isn't. But the only way you can fix it is by just being you and showing everyone you know the right way to behave. I'm not sure if you can, but try to remember that while footy is big, there are always things in your life that are bigger, and they can be good too."

Tom's eyes dropped to the ground. As he walked out on to the street and found his bike, a cold September wind ripped through him, pushing against him all the way home.

CHAPTER 06

THURSDAY

The sky had closed in around Duneldin overnight and looked like it was about to dump its contents on the town. Tom knew that this would be good for the wheat crop but not so good for the footballers, and he decided to take the side of the farmers—just for the morning.

He thought he would take his mother's advice, and focus on something else in his life that was good. He ran through a list in his head and came up pretty short. His friendships were good, but they weren't the same as what he had left behind in Melbourne; his mother loved him but was so caught up in her own life that she didn't seem too committed to his. He ate breakfast methodically, but without tasting anything, and made his usual preparations for school.

As he stepped from the verandah of his house to find his bike, he wondered if anyone would miss him if he didn't front up at all. The school's method for recording who was there and who wasn't was notoriously bad, with some kids missing multiple days at a time without anyone really noticing. Most of the time the absences were because of the necessity of working on farms and bringing harvests in, but there were stories of kids going down to the local creek and spending the day smoking and drinking then going home when school was out, with no-one any the wiser.

Jenny had left for work earlier that morning, as she did every day the paper had to be finished, so there wouldn't be any chance she would even notice Tom ride away from the school instead of towards it. He initially felt the thrill of doing something that could land him in trouble—the adrenaline powered his legs and made him go faster than he had planned. He didn't really know where he'd go or what he would do—in a town like Duneldin there weren't a lot of options for a kid who is cutting school. The main street was out, so were some of the parks. Really, all he could do was ride down to Yarramak Creek and see if he could while away his day there.

The ride took him near the part of town where Albert lived, which for a second set his mind on edge, but he discarded the thought of running into him. Soon he found himself at Casey Bridge, which was a place where a lot of the local kids jumped into the creek during summer, and where it was easy to make your way onto the track that ran parallel to the water.

He soon found a place that seemed to be made for the truanting kid—a park bench in the shade, but close enough to the water to be able to throw sticks, stones and whatever else you could find into it. The council made a big effort to keep the waterway clear, but every year as part of the annual Clean Up Duneldin Day, they pulled things out of there that made no sense. When his mum reported on it in April, she laughed when she found out they once pulled an eight-foot replica of the State of Liberty out of it. No-one knew where it came from, whose it was, or when it was dumped, but the idea of the raised torch of liberty being fished out of a muddy creek in the middle of nowhere delighted everyone's sense of the ridiculous.

Tom settled in. He took his book out of his bag and grabbed the apple he had packed for morning tea. He took a bite, flipped to his page, and happily read, losing himself in someone else's world of fire and loss for as long as he could.

It wasn't long. After about an hour he realised that there was only so much he could take of sitting by himself and reading a book. He had eaten more than he should have, and by 9.30, tried to imagine what the next six hours would involve. It dawned on him that maybe school wouldn't be so bad, and when the rain that was threatening started to fall, he got on his bike and rode as quickly as he could—without looking too desperate—to school.

By the time he got there, his hair was dripping and the back of his clothes were soaked. He went to the toilets to try and warm himself with the hand dryer, and to wait until the bell rang—walking in halfway through a lesson would bring about unanswerable questions, but if he could hide until the start of recess, then it was likely that no-one would notice that he had been missing.

In the five minutes he had to himself, he thought about the week—Albert, Mitch, biology, footy, everything—and realised that not being able to sort out how he felt was a good indication that maybe he really didn't have a role to play in how the next few days would pan out. If he did something, what would happen? Albert had made it clear that he saw Tom as not necessarily one of the enemy, but definitely a sympathiser. Tom also knew that he had never felt comfortable with the kind of ignorance that Mitch liked to throw around either. He hated the idea of sitting on a fence that was topped with barbed wire, but he didn't know what other options he had. As his mum had made clear the night before, he would be leaving the town in less than two years anyway, and without him it was going to go on as it had for the many years before he had arrived. He got the feeling that Albert was counting down the days as well, and that anyone who was young and who lived in the town would try to be on the highway and gone as soon as they could.

The bell went, and he slipped easily out of the bathroom and into the sea of students who filled the corridors, on their way to their lockers and recess. He found his locker and threw in his bag. As he shut it, Manny saw him, and skipped towards him.

"Where were you?"

"I slept in."

"Really?"

"No, not really." He smiled. "I decided I needed some time out from Duneldin, so I hopped a freight to Melbourne last night at 11, partied hard, scored some pot, listened to some grunge in Collingwood then came back on the first bus this morning. How was your night?"

"What? What are you talking about?"

"Jeez, Manny, lighten up. I wasn't going to come to school today, and now I have. I went to the creek, then got bored, and here I am."

"Okay. Did you want to hear the latest on Albert and Mitch?"

"There's a latest?"

"Yep. Apparently Mitch went around last night trying to get a bunch of people to—"

Tom knew Manny was excited because she kept taking her hair in and out of a ponytail, a twitch he kept an eye out for, if only to use for ammunition against her later.

"You know what, Manny? I actually don't want to know. I don't.

I thought about it this morning, and there's nothing I can do. Albert's right. The town is racist, but it doesn't care as long as we win on Saturday. Let's face it. There's racism everywhere. There'll be racist fans on our side screaming at the Aboriginal kids on the Masterton team, and the Masterton fans will think of every name they can to call Albert, Benny and the rest of the boys. What can you do? If you took all the racist supporters out of the crowd on Saturday then there'd be no-one watching us."

Manny stood looking at Tom, her mouth opening and closing, but saying nothing.

"Sorry. I know it's not what I was saying at the start of the week, but what am I going to do? I can't change what's happening. Mrs Thorpe taught her kids a lesson on Saturday night, and even if I don't play, or I make a speech in front of them, they're just going to head home and get re-taught the lesson. I just want to go to training tonight, make it through tomorrow, then play as well as I can Saturday. If that can happen, and I don't think about footy for four months over the summer, then that will be as good as winning the game."

"You've thought about this a bit, haven't you?"

Tom slammed his last folder into his locker. "Ruddick's lesson yesterday proved it. There's no gene for stupid, but we've all got it. Even you, even me." He shut his locker forcefully, then looked at her. He put his arm over her shoulder, then turned her towards the quadrangle. "Now let's go and dive into the shallow end of the pool of morons, shall we?"

The rest of the day plodded along, as Tom had expected. Teachers who wouldn't see the students on Friday wished them all the best for the game, and Tom sensed the beginning of nervousness in some of the players. They couldn't settle or went out of their way to make comments in class that drew attention to them. Tom felt the beginning of a knot in his stomach too, and knew that training tonight would only make things worse.

He didn't know what Fitz would have in store for them. The options were endless. Would he just treat it like any normal session, or would he do something different? He had heard stories of fireworks displays and some sort of documentary being shown, but as soon as one thing was confirmed as fact, a new rumour sprang up. Tom hoped it would just be a normal training with no type of display from anyone—laps, drills, warm down, the reading of the team and then home, just like normal.

When he arrived home after school, he was surprised to see their car in the driveway, and the kitchen light on. He unlocked the door and went inside, to find his mother sitting at the kitchen counter, sipping a cup of tea and doing a crossword. "Show of gracious behaviour, five letters, middle letter A."

"What are you doing here?"

"I'm in between jobs—tomorrow's paper is done, but I'm still working on the special edition for Saturday, Grand Final and all. How was school?"

"Oh, you know," he said, trying to notice if she knew about his absence that morning. "Fine. Learnt a bit, forgot a bit. The hype for Saturday is starting to crank up."

"Oh, good. It will give me something to write about. Any big news?"

"Nup. There are a few rumours that Fitz will do something different for the final training session, but no-one seems to have any ideas."

"Well, I guess we'll find out when we get there."

"We'll find out?" he said. "What do you mean, we'll?"

"I'm coming to watch. I figured I should not only support my son but I could get a few grabs as well—write a story about it."

"About training? Are you serious?"

"Of course. I've got eight pages to fill, and only three of them have been sold to advertisements. I'm thinking training, a few questions of people about what a win will mean to the town and then a bunch of photos. Maybe a player profile or two. What do you think?"

"I think that if we don't win, then the Saturday special edition will be used to set a few bonfires near the club early Sunday morning. Are you really coming?"

"Yes, if that's okay?"

"Course. Everyone's trying to tell us to keep it normal, but that's a joke."

He went to the cupboard and fixed himself a snack. His mother kept doing the crossword, methodically making her way through the clues, leaving only a couple unfinished. As Tom got closer to finishing his Weetbix and toast, she stood up and left the room, only to return a few minutes later, decked out in a red jumper with a black scarf wrapped around her neck, with a pair of Duneldin footy socks pulled up high over her jeans and a red beret tilted outrageously on her head. Tom snorted, and in doing so, sent a mouthful of milk up his nose. He grabbed for a tissue and tried to wipe his nose and clean up his face, but only ended up spreading his food further across his chin. Jenny laughed at him. "What?"

"Seriously? You too?"

"Of course! Have to show your support. You might want to wipe the rest of your cereal off your face, love—especially that bit in your eyebrow."

"Thanks." Tom covered his whole head with the tea towel and

rubbed indiscriminately.

"Ah, my boy," Jenny said. "A show of gracious behaviour, five letters, middle letter A. Class."

Jenny drove Tom to training, and as soon as they turned onto Gardiner Street, they knew something was different. There were streamers reaching all the way across the road, snaking along electricity wires, and red and black ribbons wound around light poles. The gates to the ground had been painted in the club colours, and even the statue recognising the service of the young men of Duneldin who fought in the World Wars—a soldier playing a bugle—had been dressed in a club jumper and had a scarf draped around his neck.

Jenny had been forced to park down the street, even though she had arrived 20 minutes early, and as the two of them made their way to the oval, they could sense the carnival atmosphere that had been created. There were barbeques, a portable bar, a raffle stand and a jumping castle for kids littered around the edge of the ground, and there were more people there than Tom could comprehend. His mother gasped when she saw the size of what had been laid on and started to write notes in the notebook she took everywhere. "Oh my," she said. "How big will it be if you actually win?"

As Tom got closer to the grandstand, he left his mother, and told her he would catch her after training, and he went into the changing rooms. The air of a celebration was there as well, and those of his teammates that had already arrived were changed, had their boots on and were raring to go, even with 15 minutes to spare. Tom remembered a time when he had been watching the news in Melbourne a few years earlier, when Hawthorn played their famous Grand Final against Geelong, and 10,000 people had turned up to watch the Hawks' final training session, and given a player a standing ovation just for running a lap as part of his comeback from serious injury. He didn't know if it would reach that level, but it seemed nonsensical all the same.

As he put his socks on, he noticed a minor hush come over the room, and looked up to see Albert enter. He was already changed and had a smile on his face that seemed to come from deep inside his happiness. He took in his surroundings, and at the top of his voice, yelled, "Bruddas! This is it! This is the shit, hey? Whoo-hoo!"

He sat down next to Tom, who sat back from where he was leaning down, and was taken aback by Albert offering a high five—Tom couldn't remember when this had ever happened before, but still slapped the offered palm. Albert leant to him and said, "You seen all those people out there? You seen 'em all? Tonight's the night, brudda, tonight's the night. I'm putting on a show." The alarm Tom felt must have registered on his face, but Albert slapped him on the leg. "Don't worry, Tom. I'm not gunna do anything, just training. No speeches, no pranks, just training the house down. Be ready, watch, and learn."

With that he stood up, and started to make his way around the room, high fiving everyone, and even joking with players Tom knew he didn't have much of a connection with. The rest of the Aboriginal boys arrived not long after Albert, and they too seemed in great spirits, a complete opposite of what had happened two days before. Tom tried to just laugh it off, but he knew that there was more to it than just a change of heart; Albert would never work like that.

At 5.10 p.m., Fitz walked into the room, and the boys quieted quickly. "Right!" he snarled. "You'll notice there's a bit of a show on in town tonight, and you might also notice that you're it! Half the town's out there, and if I'm not mistaken"—his register lowered, then rose again—"the other half are on their way! Bloody bloody!" The boys laughed out loud at his catchphrase, then again settled, waiting for what was in store. "Now tonight, it's going to be a bit of a combination of things—a few warm-ups, then some skills, and ending up with a bit of competitive work."

"Anything else?" Benny asked the question the boys really wanted answered.

"You'll see, young man, you'll see. Right. Get your mouthguards, and out you go."

The warm-up lap the boys ran together was a combination of warming up, and releasing the tension. They ran as a tight group, bumping into each other on purpose, randomly handballing footies, and trying not to trip each other over. The mindless calls of "Keep it together, boys" and "As a single team, a single team" rang out, and Tom looked up as he went around to see his mother with her camera taking photographs of them. He waved at her when he went past, and she smiled back, caught up in the feeling that was sweeping the crowd. They applauded as the team ran past, and someone suggested a second lap, just so they could get more love. They all laughed, and someone suggested the type of love they might get if they win on Saturday, and the team broke up.

Fitz used a PE teacher's whistle to call them in to the centre of the ground, and as they did, he told them to sit down in front of him, and make a semi-circle. As he did that, he pulled a cordless microphone from the pocket of his black tracksuit pants, and was heard over the PA. "Ladies and gentlemen, thanks for coming to watch the under 18s train, it's a real pleasure and something they'll remember forever. If you'd be so good as to all make your way onto the field, I have a few people here who would like to say a few words. That's right. Could you all please come on to the ground."

As the crowd came through the gates, three men in club jumpers also made their way onto the ground and made a line straight for Fitz. He shook each of their hands solemnly, and they lined up together behind the coach. Before the entire crowd had settled, Fitz began speaking. "Now I know you fellas have been having bets on what I'd come up with for the final session. I don't want to make too much of a big deal of it, but what I did want to do was introduce you to these three men. Some of you know them, and some of you will never have seen them before, but they have something in common with each other, and they want to have something in common with you. They all played in Premiership teams for the Duneldin Bombers."

The crowd started applauding, and the coach had to raise his arms to quiet them down. "I've asked each one to say a few words about what playing in a flag has meant to them, and what it might mean to you."

In Tom's mind, it was a masterstroke. Not because of what the three men said—most of which was clichéd, and had the themes of mateship, belonging and the best days of your life running through them—but more because it reminded all the people who were listening—townsfolk and players—how nostalgic footy had made them, and what the win might mean for the town in the future. Tom looked at his teammates as they were spoken to. He also saw his mum wildly taking photographs and notes, almost at the same time—but then his eyes fell on Albert. His head was up, taking in what was being said, but the turned-up mouth and raised eyebrows suggested he was hearing something a lot different than everyone else.

When the speeches finished, there was a rousing cheer from the crowd, and the president of the club made his way to the front, and called for a cheer for the men, calling them legends of the club whose names should be on every honour board in the social club. He then went on to address the players, telling them, "Boys, don't forget what was said here tonight, or how many people have turned up to watch you train. You're playing for all of us, don't forget! Do us proud!"

There was another cheer, and then Fitz retook the momentum, saying "Right, everyone, now get off the ground so they can train, will ya! We've got a game to win." The boys stood up and slapped each other on the back and ruffled each other's hair while they waited for the crowd to disperse, then Fitz grabbed the bag of footballs he carried with him, and handed out the cones. "Okay, lads, two lanes, kicks and handball receives, let's do it!"

For the next half an hour Fitz ran some basic drills that were obviously designed to get the boys moving and to get the ball in their hands, and Tom appreciated the simplicity of the thinking— they wouldn't need to do anything new to win the game given how they had played throughout the whole year, and the training was designed to let them know. Similar drills, similar result.

What was different was the next stage of training. Instead of doing what he normally did, which was run a small scratch game where the forwards played the backs, he put out two witches hats, about 10 metres from each other, and stood in the middle of them. "Right, this is it. The last drill of the year. On Sat'day, we were a bit weak in getting the ball from our opponent. In fact, there were a couple of times where we seemed to quit on the fight, and this Saturday, we cannot have that!" He emphasised every syllable, his intensity dragging the boys away from anything that might have been a distraction, including each other.

"So here we go. We get two lines on the cones. I kick the ball out, and you go one on one, battlin' each other to get it back to me. You can tackle and bump at about eighty percent, and it's got to be a legal disposal that hits me on the tit. Got it? Got it." The boys split and smiled at each other. They had done this kind of drill before, but to have it as the final hit out before the end of the session was Fitz's way of sending a message about how he wanted them to play.

Tom found himself second in line, and when it was his turn, he was pitted against Benny, who easily won the battle—he was faster than Tom and got to the bouncing ball before Tom had covered most of the required distance. Benny kicked a perfect drop punt back to Fitz, then turned and waggled a finger at him. "Ahh, Benny, he's quick too, boy. You better crank it up!" and then he laughed, and Tom did the same. He went to the back of the line and waited for his next turn.

Before that happened though, there was a ripple going through the lines. At the top of the cones stood Mitch on one side, and Albert on the other. Tom didn't know if this was manufactured or it was fate, but anticipation ran through everyone, waiting to see what would happen. Mitch stared intently at Fitz, waiting for the ball, while Albert only had eyes for the captain, checking to see which way he would move when the contest started. Fitz lobbed a ball into the air, expecting to see an aerial contest, but it never happened. Mitch elevated for the ball, but as his right foot left the turf, Albert timed a bump so perfectly that he didn't even need to leave the ground to take the mark. The hit left Mitch sprawled on the ground while Albert plucked the ball from the air one handed, and then fired a 20-metre handball to Fitz, who only nodded his appreciation.

Tom's next time up he faced Scotty, the ruckman, and this time did better. Scotty wasn't known for his skill on the ground, so when Fitz rolled a grubber towards them both, Tom made the most of his opportunity, getting down low, taking contact, then rolling with the ball before hooking a left foot kick over his shoulder that Fitz took over his head. Fitz complimented them both on their effort, and the two boys ran back to their line, nodding at each other.

Tom again turned his attention to Albert, who was making sure that he would be matched up against Mitch—this time there was no doubt. There weren't even numbers in the lines so every opponent should have been different, but there the two of them stood on the cone, waiting to go again. This time Mitch looked at Albert, and Albert beamed back at him, lifting his head in a challenge. Mitch dropped his eyes and his shoulder, and this time when Fitz kicked a grubber towards them, Mitch aimed his shoulder at the centre of Albert's chest, not even looking at the ball. It was a fool's idea. Albert moved towards the ball, then just as the impact was expected, shifted his weight so he could rock backward, almost stopping. Mitch was unable to change the angle of his attack, so went flying past Albert, missing him completely. Albert didn't miss his opportunity though and stuck a foot out so that Mitch would trip and hit the grass, hard. Albert had an easy time flicking the ball into his hand as it got to him and then kicking on his natural right foot, before running over to where Mitch was sprawled to offer him a hand up. No-one was surprised to see that the offer was rejected, and that Mitch ran back to the line with blood boiling in his neck and cheeks.

The rest of the drill seemed to fly. Tom did well each time he went out and was pleased with the way he handled the physical pressure from his opponent—but it was the Albert-and-Mitch show that people wanted to see. There were five in all, and Albert won them easily. Scotty, who had switched lines and now stood behind Tom, muttered, "Do you reckon Mitch has touched it yet?" Tom replied, "I don't know if he's even seen it, let alone touched it," and Scotty grunted in agreement.

The final contest between Albert and Mitch made everyone stop and pay attention, even those members of the crowd who hadn't been particularly drawn to the drill. Fitz fired a ball high in the air, and Albert moved to where it would drop. Mitch ran at Albert, hoping to knock him from his position and effect a spoil, but with perfect balance, strength and impossible timing, Albert put his right arm out, grabbed Mitch's jumper just below the neck and pushed him off. The intensity that it took amazed everyone, particularly Tom who knew how heavy Mitch was from previous strength sessions. When Albert took another one-handed mark and disposed of the ball perfectly with his left foot while still keeping Mitch away from his body, the team and the crowd erupted in applause. Fitz shook his head in amazement, and then yelled, "And that, ladies and gentlemen, is how to give a lesson in football. Thanks, Albert. It's been a pleasure. Now do a lap and head to the rooms, and I'll read the team." Albert waved royally, and the boys looked on in awe.

The lap they ran together lacked the positivity of the first one. They were all exhausted and emotionally washed out, but there was a pocket of the boys, led by Mitch, who kept muttering about the whole thing being a set-up, and that no-one would have beaten Albert in a game that was obviously made for him.

Tom, who had been silent up until then, felt something crack inside him, and he snapped. "That's the point, though. You couldn't beat him."

Mitch leered at Tom, and replied, "Yeah? Could you?"

Tom snorted. "Shit, no. I would have been happy just to touch it."

Mitch kept looking at Tom, even though he wasn't the topic of conversation. "And why was it only me he beat? Why wasn't it anyone else?" Tom started to answer, only to be cut off by Albert's voice coming from the back of the group.

"Genetics, mate. Genetics. Some people have good ones, some people have bad ones. Some kids have red hair, some kids freckles and some kids get made captain. It's all genetics." Some of the boys laughed, while those who weren't in the class glanced around, unsure what was going on.

"What does that even mean?"

Albert ran his way through the group, and made sure he was next to Mitch. "It means what it means. Some people are good at footy, some people are better at footy, and some people get made captain. That's all. Use your superior genes to work it out."

Mitch looked at Albert, wondering if there was a physical challenge involved, but he saw in his eyes that there was something deeper happening. He realised that a fight wasn't what Albert wanted, but something else. He said, "You'll have to ask someone else about that. I didn't ask to be captain, and I know it's annoyed you all year, but I didn't do it. Why bring it up now?"

"No reason. It'll just be fun to see what happens after the game on Saturday, that's all."

The group went silent, unsure what had just happened. Tom's gut tightened again, now sure that there was still a plan, that Albert was at the centre of it all, and the rest of the team were unwilling performers in his own private show.

The reading of the team sheet was a ritual that they normally enjoyed. Despite Albert's comments at the end of training, they gathered in the presentation room of the club to hear where they were playing. There were no big surprises in selection, other than Tom being named in the centre, when he normally lined up on either the half forward or half back flank. A few people reacted to his naming with some scandalous "Ooooohs," but everyone knew what had happened. Thanks to his move, Albert had been moved out of the centre square on the sheet, but the team knew that was a ruse too—he would start where he wanted to, as he was the best clearance player in the whole competition, let alone the team. There were no ins or outs or injuries, so Fitz read the team, the president shook all their hands as they left the room, and Tom went outside to find his mum.

She was waiting by the door, and her first question was that of a journalist. "Anything I need to know about?"

"Well, the game starts at 9 a.m. in Horminton, and we need to be at the ground no later than 8. I'll need to have my bag packed and extra food for after the game …"

"Don't be smart—although that's all important too. About the team, anything about the team?"

"No, Mum. It's as expected. We're the same as last week, except I've been named to start in the centre 'cos of the tagging job I've got. But you can't write that!" They both got in the car, and shut the doors in unison.

"What? Why not? It's team news!" Jenny started the car and pulled into the traffic making its way home.

"But we don't want them to find out about it, do we? It's meant to be a surprise."

"Oh. Right." She paused for a second, looking across. "That was a thing at the end, wasn't it?"

"What do you mean?"

"That thing between Albert and the other kid. Mitch. Was that on purpose?"

"Not until Albert made it on purpose. What did you think?"

"I didn't know what to think, but a few people around me had some interesting comments."

"Like what?"

"Like how good Albert is, and like how he'll win the game by himself if he wants to. And"—she shifted in her seat and kept her eyes on the road—"how he's a smart arse black kid who doesn't know his place."

"Oh, come on …"

"I know, I know. It was only a couple of people, but still. Now I can see what's been eating you all week."

"You didn't get it before?"

"No, I didn't. What he was doing on the field, Tom. I don't know much, but it was good, wasn't it?"

Tom paused, then spoke quietly. "It was brilliant, Mum. Mitch is a good player, sometimes better than good, but Albert destroyed him. On purpose."

"Really?"

"Yep. He did it to make a point. He'll do something else on Saturday."

"Like what?"

"No idea." They had arrived home, and Jenny made a move to get out of the car, but Tom grabbed her arm, easing her back into the seat. "So, are you going to write about it in the paper?"

"What?"

"Have an editorial that lays bare the way the town cheers for Aboriginals when they're on the field but scorns them as soon as they walk off the field. Are ya?"

"Tom …"

Tom was surprised at the rage that was boiling in him, but he couldn't hold it. He spewed it at his mother.

"Of course you aren't. The editors in Ballarat would kill you, wouldn't they? Couldn't threaten the money the paper makes by being an actual newspaper that reports what's going on, could you?"

"Tom, it's not that easy."

"Stop it, stop trying to talk down to me. You've always treated me like an adult 'cos you've had to. Now I'm acting like one, you want me to go back to being a little kid who sees the world blankly. I haven't done that for years. It's your fault and now you want to take the light out of my eyes, is that it?"

"Jesus Christ, what is this? An Inquisition? Shut up and listen, will you? I don't want to do that to you, but I can't write what you want, I just can't. You're right about the editors in Ballarat, but it's also the town. Did you see how happy people were tonight? Did you see the smiles on their faces when you ran out? Some of them were crying when those three Premiership players spoke about what playing in a Premiership meant to them, and if I unleash some massive controversy, then all that will be gone, and I can't do it."

"Then you're as bad as those fuckwits are."

There was silence. Tom knew he had gone too far but was so confused and angry he couldn't bring himself to apologise to her. He knew what was in her heart and he knew that she was right, but it didn't make him feel any better. The pressure of the whole week had finally brought its weight to bear on him—the isolation he felt, the confusion and the disgust that wrapped it all together. He exhaled roughly and opened the car door.

"Mum, I'm going inside and going to bed. I'm sorry. I shouldn't have said that and of course you aren't like them, but I'm not either. This whole thing just doesn't make any sense. You know how you told me that you'd support me leaving when I'd finished school? After tonight, I'm already on the train out of here."

CHAPTER 07

FRIDAY

Tom made his way through the school gates as the bell rang to start the school day. He had been loitering in the streets surrounding the school, waiting for the bell to ring, not wanting to see what the school would be like, and with good reason. As he walked down the hall to his locker, he couldn't avoid the black and red that had appeared overnight. Windows were covered with big pieces of black cardboard with 'Go Bombers' written on them in red, there were balloons hanging from the roof, and there were pieces of red and black crepe paper all over the floor. As Tom walked past the office, he saw an enormous poster that had been stuck to the wall. In the centre it said, 'Duneldin Primary wishes you luck for Saturday!' and it seemed like each kid at the primary school had written their name and a message. Tom felt a throb in the front of his head when he saw it and turned away from it as fast as he could. He got to his locker and left his bag without properly emptying it, just taking what he needed for the first two periods of the day.

The first ten minutes of the day was always roll call—a seemingly irrelevant part of any day where the kids sat and talked to each other and were notified of any notices that the staff wanted them to know about. Usually there was nothing of relevance, but today, Ms Hall, who Tom never saw in the school except for these ten minutes, made them all settle down as she read from the sheet.

"Today, students, there will be a special assembly held in the hall at the end of lunchtime. It will be a short ceremony, recognising a wide variety of successes that have been achieved across the school recently, and to wish the boys luck for their game tomorrow."

The students laughed at the reference to other successes, knowing that it was the principal's way of convincing the students that there was more to life than football, but they weren't fooled. As the bell to go to first period rang, and the students made their way to the door, Ms Hall stood and said, "I'd just like to wish everyone who is doing something special this weekend the best of luck. But to Tom, Ryan, Nick and Andy, particularly to you. I hope it goes well." The boys called out, "Thanks, miss," in unison, then went out to go to their first lessons.

The teachers also seemed to be aware of the feeling amongst the students—the majority of Tom's classes involved the teachers setting work that allowed them to go at their own pace: textbook work from the school's dwindling supply of resources, and a bunch of worksheets that suggested the school's two photocopiers had been punished by the staff. Even Shep, usually animated and demanding with his lessons, seemed more interested in talking about sport, and how sport linked to history. His interest seemed more international than overseas, and he told the students—the ones who were listening—about some of the more devastating sporting events that had taken place in history.

A team's plane crashing on the way to a final, an Olympics ruined by a terrorist attack, even something about a baseball team playing with the faith of 50 million people. Tom had tuned out by this stage and spent most of the lesson trying to do something that took his mind off what was going on around him. He even went as low as reading the introduction to the Shakespearean play they were studying, and surprised himself by actually getting a greater understanding of what the hell was going on with the witches and the ghosts in *Macbeth*.

Lunchtime came around too quickly. The student leadership had decided that instead of making another attempt to herald the team that they would erect a screen and a projector and show highlights from the best VFL Grand Finals of the past ten years. Tom was drawn to the idea of watching it—he was amazed that they could get the technology to do it, until someone told him they had borrowed the equipment from the football club—but decided that he would be much better off escaping, even for 45 minutes. So he did what any self-respecting social outcast would do. He went to the library.

The school library was a large, detached building at the centre of the school. There had been plans to build a mezzanine level in it at some stage, which gave it the appearance of almost being like a cathedral; its ceiling was extremely high, but obviously the funding had never come through, and the second level had never appeared. There were shelves of books around the outside of the walls, and diagonally across the huge expanse, with a handful of computers in the centre of the room. There were also plenty of corners and nooks where single desks had been placed so the senior students could work in their free periods, and it was one of these that Tom sought out. He found one easily—most of the kids were outside—and he sat with his back purposefully to the rest of the space, head down, reading a book that he had grabbed from the New and Recommended table by the librarian's desk.

It wasn't bad, but it was about the worst thing he could have chosen. After 20 pages of reading about a guy whose love for English football and Arsenal pretty much dominated and determined his life, he pushed the book away, and decided to spend the rest of the time just looking out the window, hoping inspiration would walk past him down McLean Street. As he settled into his reverie, he felt something bounce off his head, and a voice spoke softly, "Brudda, the answers are all right here in front of you, you just have to know where to look." Tom turned, and saw Albert pulling a chair over, and sitting down before he even had a chance to speak.

"Oh, hey." Tom was caught totally off guard. He hadn't expected to see Albert at all today, and now was wishing he hadn't.

"What's up? Didn't want to watch the highlights and live the joy of all those Hawks' victories in the '80s?"

"Oh, is that what they're watching?"

"Yep. All they could get was a video called *Awesome Eighties* or something, and so that's what's on."

"Sounds great. North didn't play a Grand Final at all in the '80s, so probably better that I wasn't watching." Tom was looking for any clue that might reveal how Albert was, but nothing was evident.

"Yep. How are you feeling about tomorrow?"

"All right. How are *you* feeling about tomorrow?"

"Great! Can't wait. It's a Grand Final, and I can't wait to see what happens."

"Do you still think we'll win?"

"I hope we get the result we deserve."

Tom immediately got the tone of what was being said, and he snorted. "Yeah, but what do we deserve?"

Albert smiled again, and turned his palms upward, raising his eyebrows. "Remains to be seen."

"Ha. That was a number you did on Mitch last night."

"Not really. I was just completely in the zone. Don't know what came over me."

"That's crap. You knew exactly what you were doing. The poor guy, you humiliated him."

"No, I taught him. Maybe he'll learn a lesson about how to win the footy and something good will happen to him tomorrow."

"Right, so the whole thing was you showing your concern for him? Are you sure it wasn't a guerilla response to what happened in bio?"

"Yep. I'm sure. Nothing guerilla about it, it was right there. Him being dumb enough to say out loud what he thinks had nothing to do with it. And neither did the fact the whole class, including you, brudda, just sat there and listened." Again, that enormous, cocky smile broke across Albert's face, and this time he laughed.

Tom snorted in response, and looked back out the window.

"You know, I wish we weren't playing tomorrow. I wish we'd lost on Saturday, and that all this was someone else's problem."

"Brudda, don't make me laugh. It is someone else's problem, 'cos it sure ain't yours. You're acting like all this is to do with you, when you aren't even close enough to it to smell it. What do you think will happen tomorrow? We'll win or we won't, and then on Sunday the sun will rise and we'll just move on."

"That's not true. If we win the town will go batshit insane and if we lose those people down the club will spend a lot more time than they should talking about the good old days of the 1970s and banging on about the way that things aren't what they used to be. Fitz will be crushed and I actually care about that, because he cares so much about it."

"Yeah, maybe."

"What do you think will happen tomorrow?"

"I know what's going to happen tomorrow. So do you. Shep told you in history." Albert stood up to leave.

"What do you mean, Shep told us in history? All that crap he was going on about? I didn't listen."

"You should have. It's all there."

"Yeah, but …" Albert turned to walk away, but Tom stood up and grabbed his shoulder, turning him back. "Albert, what the fuck? You can't just drop these stupid hints and then leave. You're not in a murder mystery. People really care about this. Even you."

"Yeah, but I care for different reasons, and they matter more than the scoreboard. I think you do too, but you can't really do anything about it. I can. See you at assembly."

When the bell rang to end lunch, Tom picked up the book he had been reading, put it back on the New and Recommended table, and thanked the librarian. He made his way back towards his locker, and then realised he was swimming against a strong tide—every kid in the school, from the year 7s all the way to the seniors, was heading to the gym for the special assembly. Tom turned around to mix in with the flow of humanity and found himself moved along effortlessly until he reached the open double doors.

The gym had been transformed into an auditorium, with rows of plastic chairs put out. The staff were directing kids to sit in their year groups, with the year 11s towards the back—the youngest sat at the front and the eldest at the rear—and Tom was reminded about the size of the school. About 400 kids filled the hall, and when the staff filed in the number hit closer to 450. This was nothing like the school that he had been at in Melbourne, which had almost 900 students, but he was still impressed, given the size of the town. He found a seat with the rest of his year group, and as soon as he sat down, Manny scooted over from her seat and sat next to him. "Hey," he said, and she bumped shoulders with him in greeting. "Where were you?" she asked.

"You mean at lunchtime? I was hiding."

"From what?"

"Everything. What did you do?"

"Sat in the quad and watched the highlights. You know we're a Hawks family—I couldn't miss the chance. I reminded quite a few people who might have forgotten how good we are."

"How could they forget? You won it at VFL Park last year!"

"That's true, but you have to do what you can. Things aren't looking good this year though."

"Better than us. We're where we'll always be, middle of the ladder. The curse of the North supporter. How was the vibe? Are people excited about tomorrow?"

"You bet. Everyone's talking about carpooling and how they're getting home, and someone's trying to organise an after-party."

"The game starts at 9 and will be done by 11! The after-party could start at 2 in the rotunda at Civic Park and we'd still all be home to watch *Hey Hey It's Saturday*."

"Come on, you know what we're like—any chance to have a party. People are pressuring Mitch to have it 'cos he's the captain and needs to show leadership."

Tom snorted and rolled his eyes. "That's leadership?"

"Well, are you offering?" She turned to him. "Hey, that's a great idea. Why don't you have the party? Your house would be great for it. You could go from being that weird kid who hides all the time to being that weird kid who let everyone get drunk in his backyard."

"Sounds tempting but I'm not sure Jenny would approve. She spends every Monday morning meeting with the police to find out about what happened on the weekend and what she can write about—not sure how she'd feel if she had to write about herself."

"Anyway. Are you ready to be adored? Again?"

"What, this? Not really. It's a wank—it's so obviously about footy, but Joycey will want to try and be inclusive. Watch the chess club get a mention, and the four kids who play musical instruments."

With that, the principal, Ms Joyce, stood up to the microphone, and began her address. In her clipped, almost off-putting manner, she spoke of the importance of recognising all types of achievement, be it academic, musical or sporting, and that there were never too many times to do this. Tom nudged Manny every time she mentioned parts of school life which would normally draw ridicule—his favourite was the triumph of the sculpture club in completing the creation of a series of pencils that would stand outside the school and represent their values. She then asked all the students she named to stand and be recognised for their achievements. It took her 15 minutes to make her way through the list, and by the end of it, about a quarter of the school was standing up.

She left the football team until last. "Now I know that these young men do not represent the school per se, but I did want to wish them all the best for the game tomorrow. Regardless of the outcome we will all be exceedingly proud of you and wish you all the best. I, the school and the town are all behind you and can't wait to celebrate your victory at school on Monday. Would the following students also stand up?"

She went on to read out the team sheet. Not all of the boys

were there—some boarded at schools in Ballarat and travelled home on the weekend—but most of them were present. As Tom rose to his feet he looked around for his teammates, and saw them standing—some were laughing, some were reluctant, while others were trying not to do anything that made them look stupid. Tom locked eyes with Albert, who was one of the last to stand, and he had a look on his face that reminded Tom of a comedian who had a really good joke, but was purposefully hiding the punchline.

Ms Joyce asked the school to give everyone standing a round of applause, which they did. They then all stood to sing the national anthem and were dismissed. The students slowly filed out, knowing that the longer they took to leave the shorter the next period would be, but eventually Tom found himself sitting in double maths, working on every second question from the left-hand side of the textbook. The repetitive thoughtlessness helped get him through the rest of the day. When the bell went, he couldn't wait to get himself out of the school and home, where at least he could let his imagination run wild without him trying to stop it.

He got home, dumped his bike in the garage and threw his helmet on top of it. He fished his key from under the pot plant, unlocked the back door—a throwback to his time living in the city; people in the town found it almost insulting that they thought they would ever be burgled—and went inside. He did not expect his mother to be home, what with the knowledge that she had a special edition to get out the next day, but it was obvious that she had been there during the day. There was a teacup and an empty bread plate sitting on the kitchen counter, and next to that was a manila folder, with TOM scrawled on it.

Tom picked it up and walked to the fridge, trying to open both the folder and the door at the same time. As part of this impossibility, he dropped the manila folder, and its contents spilled all over the floor. Tom was taken aback by what he saw. There were striking glossy photos of the boys training, specifically A lbert, Benny and the other Aboriginal boys. One photo particularly grabbed Tom—it was of Albert in the middle of a drill. His feet weren't touching the ground, and his body looked like it was moving in three different directions at the same time—his eyes were looking right, his hands aimed left, while his hips were perfectly situated about his feet, so that when he landed he could go whatever way he desired. Tom quickly gathered up the papers and slammed the fridge door shut with his bum. He moved to one of the stools, laid the pages out and made his way through them.

Amongst all the articles about the team selection, the Grand Final and the impact the game would have on the town, both socially and economically, there was one that purely focused on the Aboriginal players—it had a short biography on each one of them, discussing their backgrounds and history, and two paragraphs that wrapped up the article that discussed the importance of Indigenous players in football. It mentioned names like Syd Jackson, Maurice Rioli and the Krakouer brothers, and then referred to all of the local boys, particularly Albert, in the same breath as those famous VFL players.

He read, "It is absolutely crucial to understand the long-standing impact that the Indigenous culture has had on our game, and it is *our* game. Everyone's. Not white, not black, not Asian, but everyone's. When the Bombers win today, they win for the whole of Duneldin. All of us will remember it, not just those who think they have an exclusive right to enjoy the pleasures that the game brings." His heart swelled, and he threw down the pages.

He didn't know what would happen to his mum when the town read the closest thing she would ever come to an editorial, but he knew that she knew what she was doing, and that she had written it for him.

The screen door slammed, and Jenny came in, flinging her bag onto the chair nearest the door. "Tom?"

"Yep. In the kitchen."

"Did you read it?"

"Yep. You're a legend." He went to her, and threw his arm around her, and hugged her. She laughed and rested her head on his shoulder.

"Too much?"

"Nah. It's great. And it's in the right spot too—right near the end of an article a lot of people will have trouble reading anyway. Are you worried about it?"

"Nup. If anyone wants to have a go at me about it then I'll just let them and I'll move on. It's worth it."

Tom picked up the pages and re-read the rest of the articles and flicked through the photos. He put them back in the envelope and walked to the cupboard. "I'll cook tonight, shall I?"

"Yes, you shall. Pasta again?"

"Pasta again. Might do a vegetable though, just to show off." Tom started rummaging for saucepans and utensils in the drawers, and his mother sat down, heavily.

"Jesus, what a week."

"Yep. And it's not over. Got to get through tomorrow, then it's done. Are you writing it up?"

"No, the guys in Horminton are going to. I can just come and watch."

"Well, hopefully there'll be something worth writing about.

Plenty of Grand Finals have been over before the ball is even bounced. This one might too."

"You reckon?"

"No, but I think the biggest battle will actually be within our team. Something's happening. I don't think the Aboriginal boys will turn up."

"What? They'll have to."

"You'd think so. I can't work out what else they'd do. Albert is so smart, he'll have something planned to get him out of trouble."

"Holy shit! Tom!"

"What? Are you worried about the footy too?"

"No, not the footy. Check the saucepan—it's burning!"

CHAPTER 08

SATURDAY 6.00 a.m.

At his mother's suggestion, Tom had tried to go to bed early—they would need to be up at a ridiculous hour to get organised, eat, get in the car and then drive the 45-minute trip to Horminton to make the time set by Fitz for the arrival.

The game had been planned to start at 9 a.m. so that the reserves could finish their game in time to allow the seniors to begin at 2.30 p.m., allowing the whole season to be wrapped up in one place and on one day. Tom didn't mind the early time—he wanted to avoid hanging around for the whole day waiting for it to start, but at 11.30 on Friday night when he was still trying to get himself to sleep, he found himself cursing anyone and anything for setting the program.

He tried turning the pillow over, sleeping at opposite ends of the bed, reading—anything he could think of to get to sleep, and when he finally did, he found himself waking up and turning over, looking at his clock, fearing that he'd slept through his alarm and would be late for the game. He knew they would have to leave no later than 7 a.m., but when he rolled over again at 6, he said to his pillow, alarm clock and the rest of his room, "Right. That's that then," and swung his legs out of bed.

The bruise on his arm was still sore. He had iced it and looked after it as much as possible and he followed the advice of the club, but still when he prodded it he felt a bolt of pain shoot through him, so in desperation he decided to wrap it, hopefully protecting it from any serious contact he would face. Creeping into the bathroom to find the medical chest, he succeeded in tripping over the towel he had left on the floor the night before and crashing into the vanity. He looked around, scared that he had woken his mother up, but after he had counted to fifteen and didn't hear anything he breathed out and crouched down to look through the cupboard to see if they had any bandages. When he stood up, he reflexively screamed—his mother's reflection appeared in the mirror, hair dishevelled and eyes red. She too started screaming at him to be quiet, and for five seconds there was a combination of noise and fear that ended by them both looking at each other in the mirror, and with hands raised, telling the other to calm down. When they had, Jenny spoke first. "Oh my God Tom. What are you doing up? We don't have to leave for almost an hour."

"I know. I just kept rolling over and looking at the clock, and then about ten minutes ago I realised it wasn't worth trying to go back to sleep. My arm still hurts, and I was going to tape it."

"Okay. Did you get any sleep?"

"A bit. Not as much as I should have. I'm going to be knackered before I even run out."

"You'll be right. The adrenaline will get you through to after the game, then you can sleep as much as you want. When you win though, you'll ..."

"Oh come on, Mum. Don't curse me!"

"What?" Jenny was sorting through the fishing tackle box that doubled as a medicine chest, and had started to unravel a bandage. "I just said you'd win. What's wrong with that?"

"That's the last thing you should say to me. You can't be overconfident and go around thinking you'll win. You have to be the underdog and imagine you're up against it."

"That's ridiculous. You've won every game this year and the team you're playing against are …"

"Mum! I know! Everyone knows!" Jenny had grabbed Tom's arm and had it over her shoulder and was starting to wind the bandage around it. She went up and down his arm to the elbow, and by the time he had finished talking, she had completed the job.

"You just can't talk about it. Nice work, by the way."

"Thanks. Is it too tight?"

Tom flexed his arm and shook his head no.

"Great. I'll just tape over the end of the bandage and hopefully that will get you through the game. I had no idea you were so superstitious."

"I'm not, it's just one of those unwritten rules."

"Right. Okay. Come and sit down, and you can tell me a few more of them. Maybe I'll publish a book called *The Unwritten Rules of Football*. It'll sell a million."

They ate breakfast together, with Jenny doing everything she could to keep the conversation light. She had asked about the stupidity of football, the high school gossip and who was going out with who, and the plans she was trying to make for him for the next lot of school holidays, which would start a week after the season finished. After 15 minutes of it, Tom took his mother's hand, and looked at her. "Mum. I love you, and I know what you're trying to do, but can you please just shut up? No matter how much you try, I can't stop thinking about the game. You could tell me anything you want about whatever you want, and I would probably just nod. Okay?"

Jenny laughed. "Okay. But will we go back to being normal when the game finishes?"

"Hard to say. Depends how the game finishes, I suppose." Tom looked at her with a rueful grin, and she smiled back.

"Just do your best and try to enjoy yourself. What else can you do?"

They had packed everything the night before and had what they needed by the front door—Tom's footy bag, a canvas bag full of food and a deck chair for Jenny to sit on during the game. There was also a rug and a thick coat, but the weather looked fine, and the crispness of a late winter's day greeted them when they looked out the window. Jenny went into her room to find her keys and handbag. She came back to the hall to find Tom rummaging through his bag. "What are you doing? We packed it all last night and checked it."

"I know. I just wanted to make sure."

"Tom! There's nothing to make sure of. Your boots are clean, your shorts are in there and we even checked how well your socks are rolled. I watched you scrub your mouthguard and put it in the pocket inside the bag. No-one touched it overnight. You're going to give yourself an anxiety attack if you keep doing this. Just grab it and get in the car."

"I know, I know."

"Get in the car, and let's go. We'll be late."

They walked to the car, and just as he reached the door, Tom jolted. "Music! Have we got music?"

"Yes. Your favourite tape is in there. Look, given it's the Grand

Final, I'll even let you listen to it without criticising it."

"Right. Great. Thanks."

They had imagined that the trip to Horminton would take about 45 minutes, but had left a bit earlier than they had planned, thanks to Tom waking up so early. Despite this, they only just got to the gates of the ground on time—the road between Duneldin and Horminton had been stacked with cars. Every road that joined the highway seemed to have cars lining up, and the convoy between the two towns gave the impression that there was no-one actually left living there. In fact, most of the shops had stayed closed. The supermarket and the petrol station were manned by one or two workers, and places like the butcher and the newsagent simply had signs in the window that said 'Go Bombers!'. That was enough to tell people they wouldn't open again until Monday morning. If you were a criminal then it would be a great place to start a crime spree, but this problem was avoided because even those in the town with a mind for theft had gone to the game.

Jenny had stayed just under the speed limit the whole way to Horminton because she had to. The single-lane highway that joined the two towns didn't allow for a lot of overtaking, and she would only be pulling out to pass another car that was driving to the game. Tom looked behind him and noticed that the principal of the school, Ms Joyce, was behind her, wearing a Bombers beanie and with a red and black scarf hanging out of the window. He was pretty sure that the car in front was Benny and his family— they drove an old Subaru that always looked as if it had been washed in a mud bath, with a Ningaloo Reef sticker on the back. Tom spent the majority of the trip looking at the sticker and wondering how exactly a family from the centre of Victoria went to the Ningaloo Reef, a welcome respite from all the other things that could have gone spinning through his head.

Jenny sat mostly in silence—she realised that Tom wouldn't be in the mood for much of a conversation and, as she promised, sat through an eclectic selection of grunge music that Tom described as "highly motivational", although to her it sounded like a series of angry suicide notes, one after the other. She wondered what motivation could be gained from a group of young people supposedly singing about the eternal drudgery of their lives, but she let it go. She also knew that any effort by her to try to give Tom some perspective about the game would be wasted, an idea that was only reinforced when they turned into Baker Street, where the Civic Oval Reserve was located.

It sat amongst an impressive Botanical Gardens and was hemmed in by the Wimmera River, but the natural beauty was not what Jenny was struck by—it was the amount of traffic and people that had converged on the ground, even at ten to eight, and the efforts that Horminton had gone to to promote the games. Flags and banners flew from every light pole and street sign, and words like 'Go Hawks', 'Pies for Premiers' and 'The Lions Rule' had been spray-painted across the asphalt.

The entrance to the oval, where parents had been assured there would be parking for players' families, was choked with people, and everywhere they looked Tom and Jenny recognised people they knew lining up to get in. Jenny crawled to the gate, wound her window down and handed over a ticket that had been provided to the players' families to the old man standing on the gate, and was waved to a section of the car park that was surrounded by traffic cones. She found one of the last remaining parks and, almost before she stopped, Tom had unbuckled his seat belt and opened the door, ready to run to the change rooms. Jenny had to wrench the handbrake to bring the car to an abrupt stop as a way of getting his attention. "Tom!"

"Yeah? What?"

"The car hadn't even stopped. Calm down!"

"Yeah, right. Sorry, Mum. Gotta go." Jenny grabbed his arm and held tight.

"No, you don't. You're right on time. Just look at me." Tom did and saw his mother smiling. "Have a great time. You'll do really well, I know it. It'll be fun."

"Shit, Mum. This game is going to be a lot of things, but one thing it won't be is fun."

He pushed the car door shut and made his way through the human traffic to the change rooms that were under the grandstand. They had been told which side to go through and what to expect, but still Tom felt apprehensive making his way towards the entrance. He felt relieved when he saw Frank Collins standing at the small door next to a staircase welcoming the players and officials in. As Tom approached, Frank stuck out his enormous hand—the fingers were like fat sausages, and they surrounded Tom's. "Good luck today, Tom," he said gravely. "Do your best, and I know we'll be proud."

"Thanks, Frank. I'll do what I can."

"Good boy, good boy."

Tom walked past him and into the rooms.

The first thing he noticed was how normal it all seemed. The room, despite its size, seemed exactly the same layout as the change room at Anzac Park in Duneldin, down to the signs on the wall and the location of the warm-up benches. He looked for some familiar faces and saw them everywhere—most of the players had already arrived and were in the processes of getting strapped and changed, and as Tom moved to the centre of the room, he was greeted by Fitz, who, like Frank, felt the need to shake his hand.

"Good to see you, Tom. How're you feeling?" Tom started to answer, but before he could say anything, Fitz continued. "Good, good. Ready for your job? Good. The kid's actual name is Danny Thompson. Not sure if you need to know that, but anyway. I just want you to call him number 9 today, all right? They've named him on the wing but we're sure he's going to start in the guts. Doesn't matter where he lines up, just go to him. When you do …" Tom's mind immediately shifted to what Albert had been telling him about tagging a left footer, and then to the plan he had formulated for himself. He didn't tell Fitz what it was, not because of the potential stupidity of it, but because he had completely tuned out. It took Fitz saying in his ear, "Tom. Tom? Tom!" to get him to refocus.

"Yes, Fitz. I'm ready. It's all good."

"Good. Then get changed before we head out to warm up."

Tom did what he was told. George, the club physio, strapped his ankles for him, and looked at the tape on his arm, raising an eyebrow when he did. "My mum did it. It's all good," Tom said, and George shook his head, bemused. "Sure it is. Come and see me at half time when it falls off and I'll redo it."

Once George had moved on to the next player, Tom sat with his back against the wall, breathing deeply, trying to take everything around him in. It seemed to be both moving quickly and at a snail's pace at the same time. He ticked off in his head who was there and who wasn't—he realised that the majority of the team had already arrived, and that despite his organisation, he had been one of the last.

As he looked to the door, he saw Albert arrive, a smile beaming across his face. He raised an eyebrow to Fitz as a way of greeting and he gave Tom a thumbs-up as he made his way to his seat. Tom's initial feeling was relief, but then the apprehension returned. Just because Albert was here didn't mean anything, except that his major theory had been wrong, and Tom's foreboding wasn't relieved by the easy manner in which his friend now went through his pre-match preparation.

After five or so minutes, Fitz blew a whistle, and called out, "We're heading out for a warm-up in two minutes, boys—a quick lap of the oval, a few drills and then back inside for the last part of our preparation. Let's go!" The players stood up and moved into the centre of the room, slapping each other on the back and high fiving. When Fitz yelled, "Come on!" they moved towards the entrance, and into the sunshine.

The crowd was not in place for the game yet—it wasn't meant to start for half an hour, but even so there were enough people to give them a round of applause as they made their way over the short distance between the rooms and the oval, and it took everything Tom had not to look around him to see who was there. He had been told by pretty much everyone that they were coming. He had doubted it originally; now he was more than assured that the whole town would be watching. They made their way around the ground as a team, and the first thing Tom noticed was the odd shape of the ground—it was shaped like a square with two semi-circles at each end, to create an almost perfect oblong, down to the fact that the boundary line between the two 50-metre arcs were dead straight lines, with no hint of a curve. Tom had no idea what this would mean for either team given that neither had played there throughout the year, but he imagined himself just running straight lines the whole day parallel to the boundary, chasing his opponent and kicking the ball long and deep to his team's forwards. The ground seemed longer than normal too—the distance between the 50-metre lines and the centre square was at least 10 metres, and he immediately knew this was to their benefit. They were a quick team, and with Albert bursting out of the middle with room to move, he began to see the way that the shape of the ground would work to their advantage.

The team's runner, Steve Parsons, then called them to the river end of the field, and they started doing lane work, just to get the ball into their hands. Most of the players seemed over eager and were charging at the ball and making obvious mistakes that showed their nerves, but Albert was the picture of calm. He didn't drop the ball or miskick the entire time, and the runner kept reminding the rest of the players to take his lead. They soon settled, and by the time they had finished the drills and made their way off the ground and back to the change rooms, the team had relaxed, and were actually starting to feel like it might just be another game.

Time now seemed to be racing and Tom noticed the rising intensity in every interaction he had. Everyone was high-fiving and back slapping, some boys were butting heads and yelling. Tom was trying to control his breathing, but couldn't. His heart was beating faster than normal, and his eyes were whirling, constantly moving from face to face. He tried to rationalise his actions, but couldn't. He had a growing desire, thanks to the escalation in the room, to get out onto the ground and just run, regardless of what happened in the process.

Fitz, of course, had other ideas. As soon as the crescendo

seemed to peak, he gathered them at one end of the shed, sitting in a horseshoe shape with a single chair in the middle. They sat together, almost on top of one another, legs slapping, and Fitz came and sat down. He took a piece of paper from his pocket, glanced at it, then screwed it into a ball and threw it on the floor.

"Now boys," he started. "There's not much to say. I can tell you as much as I like that this is just another game, but we all know that's bullshit." The boys raised their eyebrows, and looked at each other—Fitz notoriously never swore to them as a group. "This is a Grand Final, and for some of you, it'll be the only one you ever play. The rest of your footy careers, be they long or short, will be about trying to get back here, and some of you, no matter what, never will. That's why you need to look at each other right now and make a promise to each other. No matter what bloody happens out on that field today, no matter what anyone says to you or does to you, when you come off the ground you make sure you can look your teammates in the eye and say to them I did everything I could! I gave every single piece of myself to you, to our jumper and to this team, and I did whatever I could to win! I ran as hard, I tackled as hard, I took as many bloody hits as I could! You can't put a price on what you'll do out there today, but here's the question you have to keep running through your head—what's it worth to you? What's it worth?"

He had started yelling now, and was out of his seat, which tipped over given the violent way he stood up. "Is it worth being exhausted, being hurt, putting on that last shepherd, that last bump, running that last metre to support your mates? What's it worth? Is it worth the pain you'll feel at the end if we lose, or is it worth the feeling of glory and satisfaction we're going to have when we drive back down the highway to the celebration tonight with that bloody cup in our hands as Premiers? What's it worth, boys, what's it worth?"

His volume and intensity infected the boys and, without thinking, they all stood up and started chanting, "What's it worth, what's it worth?" Even Albert got up and had wrapped his arms around some of his teammates, and was chanting. Tom was yelling it now and just as the noise started to reverberate around the change room to the point of becoming painful, Fitz stood on his chair and yelled, as loudly as he could, "Now get out there and show 'em! Show 'em what it's bloody worth!" and with that the boys charged out of the room and onto the field.

CHAPTER 09

SATURDAY 8.55 a.m.

Both teams had entered the field to a cacophony of sound—Tom felt like a wall of some kind had hit him when he ran out. It only added to the sense of drama he felt was going to reveal itself on the field. The team lined up to run through their banner—a huge black sheet of crepe paper with an enormous red sash over it and a sign that read 'The Bombers Are Landing' in huge red letters that made Tom feel like he was on a ground much larger and well removed from the Western Districts of Victoria.

The team smashed through it, with Tom staying somewhere near the back, fearful of tripping over and making an idiot of himself. He got through it easily, and the two teams—Masterton had come on to the ground minutes before Duneldin—lined up for the national anthem. Tom wondered if it was going to be sung by a local B-grade celebrity, but it seemed the league's budget didn't stretch that far. The opening notes rang out of a tinny set of speakers on top of the grandstand, and the players sang in a monotone that could only be heard by people standing within a few metres. The two groups broke after that and did a quick handball drill while the captains met and tossed the coin. Mitch jogged back to the group, pointing to the river end. He called the group together—

they wrapped arms around each other, while Mitch yelled words that were supposedly motivational at them, but all Tom heard was a kid screaming the clichés that he had heard all season. He looked for Albert. He was looking at each of the Aboriginal boys, making sure he held their eyes for a second before nodding, and when the group broke, Albert went to each one of them, slapping them on the back, speaking quickly to them. Tom tried to hear what he was saying but couldn't. As the players broke and went to their positions, Tom finally caught up to him.

"You ready?"

"Yeah, brudda, sure am."

"Still think our best is better than their best?"

"Sure do, brudda. I'm going to give the town what it deserves today, you watch me. You ready?"

"Yep. I've got two plans. The one you gave me and the one I came up with."

"Oh yeah?" They were now inside the centre square, and number 9 was making his way in, as Fitz had predicted.

Albert put his arm around Tom's shoulder. "Are you going to have a go at him?"

"No, I'm just going to talk."

"Talk? What are you going to say to him?"

Tom smiled and punched Albert on the arm. "I'm going to politely introduce myself and then start a conversation about books."

"What?"

"Yep. Wonder if he's a reader."

"You're nuts."

"Yep. And by the end of the game, hopefully he will be too."

Tom broke away from Albert, and went to number 9, a tall but solid dark-haired boy, with thick legs and wide hips. Tom stood next to him and extended his hand. Surprised, and more out of reflex than desire, Danny Thompson took it. Tom held it tightly and shook vigorously.

"Nice to meet you, Danny. I'm Tom. You're going to get to know me fairly well today."

"Shut up, mate. Why'd they put you on me? Aren't you just a plodder?"

"I get good money as a babysitter. I think they're paying me three bucks an hour to mind you." The two boys were now side by side, bumping and jostling.

"We'll see."

"Hey, do you like to read?"

"What?" Thompson turned to Tom, incredulous.

"Actually, can you read? I wasn't sure. I'm guessing you can. I'm reading this great book at the moment; it's called *Fahrenheit 451*. You'd love it. I'm gonna tell you about it today. It's about people setting stuff on fire."

"Shut up."

"There's this guy called Montag, and he's a fireman, right? But the weird thing is, he sets stuff on fire, instead of putting it out."

The teams were now in place, and Tom kept nattering. The umpire rolled the ball in his hands, looking around to make sure the right number of players were on the field and that there were only four inside the centre square. Once he was happy, and with an obvious pause for dramatic effect, he held the ball in the air, waited for the siren, and the game was on.

When they ran into the huddle at the end of the first quarter, there was a feeling amongst them that something was wrong. The scoreboard didn't show it—they were up by 10 points having kicked 3.6 to 2.2, but it was the way they were playing that was unsettling. They made mistake after mistake and had kept the opposition in the game. Tom was happy with how he was doing his job—Thompson had had two handballs and a misdirected kick. Tom had described the first 40 pages of his book in excruciating detail while also getting a couple of useful possessions. The Masterton players had kept trying to block Tom, but so far hadn't been able to do it effectively enough and there had been times when Thompson's frustrations at being so effectively shut out of the game were obvious.

Beyond this, Tom was starting to feel like there were forces at play he couldn't understand, and they revolved around Albert. He had plenty of the ball but seemed unsure of himself, having been tackled a couple of times and been forced to kick under pressure, something Tom could not remember ever happening. There had been one brilliant passage—the ball had gone from end to end, started and finished by Albert with only the team's Aboriginal players touching the ball in what seemed like a predetermined set play, but otherwise, he had been largely absent and it was the team's lesser lights who were keeping them in front.

Fitz called them into the huddle, and while the boys drank and sprayed themselves with water, he calmly spoke to them. "Boys, the thrill's over. Yep, we're in a big game, yep, the crowd is enormous and yep, the opposition is good, but not that good. What are we doing? Remember the basics. First option, kick long to the hot spot and use the speed and the space. We're a ten-goal better side than them but it looks like we're trying to keep it interesting. The only thing that should interest us is grindin' them into the bloody dirt! Albert?"

"Yes, boss?" Albert was standing at the back of the huddle with two of the other Aboriginal boys, intensely discussing something, and pointing to positions on the ground.

"I need you to get involved! You've been running around like a lost boy out there, and when you've had it, you've wasted it. Any problems?"

"No, boss."

"Okay."

"Yes, boss." Albert's smile and laconic nature lit a fire in Fitz's eyes, and he was obviously trying to hold his anger back. Albert smiled at him again and raised a thumb, but Fitz had moved on to giving other instructions. Tom made his way through the group to where Albert was standing, a smirk on his face.

"How's it goin'?" Tom tried to keep his voice light and hoped he wouldn't betray his concern.

"Great! I mean, we're up by ten points in a Grand Final and I'm learning all about an insane book. How you doin'?"

"Good. I mean, I would be if we were playing better. You okay? You look slow."

"Everyone seems worried about me. It's heartening. I'm good. Don't worry about me, brudda, I'm plannin' on puttin' on a show in the second half."

"The second half, why then?"

"Why not?"

The siren to restart the game had rung, and the players returned to their positions. Tom noticed that his opponent was making his way to the forward pocket, and as a result, he followed, pointing to the bench to let them know as he headed towards him. Fitz yelled, "Yep. Robbo. Go to a wing. Mitch. Get in the guts. Albert, you're up!"

Tom raced down to the back pocket, feeling better about not

having to be at the centre bounce, but also wondering how long it would be until Thompson moved back up the ground. He went to him, placed his arm across his opponent's, and started talking. "Hey, Danny, or is it Daniel? Dan? Not that it matters. It's around this time that we find out that Montag's been hiding books in his roof. The roof! Can you believe it? He's actually …"

With this, the siren rang and Thompson bolted towards the wing as fast as he could go—it was an obvious ploy to try and break Tom's tag. Tom ran a couple of steps behind him and tried to catch up. He was almost there, when he saw a flash of blue come out of the corner of his eye, and felt his shoulder burst and his head jerk back. His elbow, which he had just tucked into his chest at the same time as the hit, crushed against his ribcage, and every bit of air was forced from his stomach. There was a sound that somehow reminded him of a car crash and, before he could comprehend why, he found himself on the ground, listening to the angry roar of the crowd, unaware of why the sky was now closing in around him, and how clouds had found their way inside his head.

When he came to, his head was throbbing, and he was hardly able to stand up. He was being helped from the field by two trainers, and there was blood running out of his nose and onto his jumper. He tried to wipe it off but found that he wasn't able to coordinate his hand to his face, and he somehow smeared it all over himself. He was taken to the bench where, after he sat down, the trainers applied an ice pack to his lip, and pushed his head back. Someone wrapped a blanket around him, and he closed his eyes. The rest of his senses were still functioning, and all he could hear coming from the crowd was anger. Calls of "Gutless prick! Dirty! Disgraceful! Coward!" filled the air, and Tom wondered what they were describing.

It hadn't occurred to him that the crowd were referring to what had happened to him, and that the energy that now seemed ready to jump the fence and strangle the game was in reaction to him being shirtfronted 40 metres away from where the ball was.

Fitz strode over to him and got down on his haunches. "Mate. Tom. Mate, are you okay?"

"S'pose. My head hurts a bit."

"What's the score?"

"The what?"

"The score."

"No idea. There's a score?"

Fitz stood up and walked away. "Right, so he's off for a while. Refit the midfield so that Albert's got space and tell Benny he needs to go to number 9 and shut him down. No retaliation, just hurt him if there's a tackle."

Tom kept trying to put his head down so he could watch the game, but it kept being forced back by the trainers, so they could keep the ice on and stop the bleeding. After a couple of minutes it did, and Tom began to get clarity back. As he held a piece of coarse paper towel to his nose and watched the game, he started to remember where he was and what he was doing there. He now knew he'd been targeted—he even had an idea of who it was, and how it had happened. He knew Fitz would not let him back on the field this quarter, but he also knew that he was determined to go back on and do his part. He was not revengeful by nature but he wanted to do something to show that he wasn't afraid of what had happened, and that he could still make his mark on the game.

By being off the field though, the game had shifted in its balance. The changes in position had unsettled them, and the players were furious about what had happened. Masterton had started to get on top and were making more of the errors that Duneldin continued to make—missed tackles, wayward handballs and shocking kicking had meant that the scores were now only two points the difference, and that it was a chance that they would go into halftime behind.

The last two minutes of the half were telling. Twice the Duneldin backline held against a Masterton attack, and twice they coughed up handballs in the centre of the ground as they made their way forward. With about 30 seconds left to go, and the ball in the Masterton forward line, Albert grabbed the ball in a contest—literally grabbed it out of his opponent's hand without him even knowing what had happened, then fired a 20 metre handball without looking to Jordan Burke, who was in space on the wing. Jordy's eyes lit up, and he turned and ran as fast as he could for goal, taking a bounce and then kicking it long to a contest. Dunedlin's stocky full forward, Jason, one out in front of the goal square, edged his opponent under the ball then twisted back and ran onto the bouncing ball, slamming it through, seconds before the siren rang. The celebration amongst Tom's teammates was euphoric, but Tom kept his eyes on Albert. Benny had gone to him and raised his arms, and Albert raised a hand, in what appeared to be regret. Tom's eyebrows raised, wondering what it was that Albert felt the need to apologise for.

The goal seemed to release a valve for the team, and as they came together to walk off, there were signs amongst them that they now had the game for the taking. Boys yelled, "We've got 'em!" or "It's ours now!", and their heads were raised and shoulders back, feeling that whatever Masterton threw at them, they'd be able to take it.

Fitz wasn't so sure. As soon as they had entered the room and got a drink, he ran around the room, yelling, "Out! Get everyone out. All I want in here is the players! Everyone else can wait their bloody turn to talk to them. After the game. Get everyone out!"

Frank Collins, who had been quietly standing in the corner of the change room when the boys came in, sprang into action, shooing everyone who wasn't a player—and Tom marvelled at how many people had got into the rooms at half time—out the door.

Tom looked for his mother, knowing she'd be worried about him getting cleaned up, but she wasn't to be found. He was feeling better. There was a dull ache in the back of his head and the bruise on his arm was more tender than it had been at the start of the game, but he was determined to go back on, and he committed to not letting on how badly he had felt. He had a bit more of a sense of who had hit him. He remembered a blond, long-haired flash coming at him from the corner of his eye, and knew it could only have been one of two players. He wasn't going to retaliate or target anyone, he just knew he wanted to be able to walk off the ground, find the kid who hit him, then just point to the scoreboard, knowing that the pain in his head would go away, but the pain of losing a Grand Final never would.

Fitz's voice once again dragged him back. "Right, boys." There was a low foreboding in his voice now. Not anger or fury, but something worse: disappointment. "I'm not going to rant and rave. There's no point. All I know is we're a ten-goal better team than these clowns, but we're only eight points up. I noticed you getting pretty excited when we came off the ground, but you've gotta remember, they're closer to us than they should be, and they probably think they've got a sniff. We've got to kill that thing they've got. That hope. Kill it. It's easy. Just beat them everywhere.

Beat 'em in the air. Beat 'em on the ground. When you tackle them, imagine you're grinding them into the ground. You saw what they did to Tom."

Tom noticed every eye turn to him, and Basher, who was sitting next to him, ruffled his hair. "Tom's going back on this quarter." The team roared their approval. "He's been doing his job. Doing it so well that some bastard cleaned him up so he couldn't do it no more." The team again yelled Tom's name. He started to blush at the attention, but Fitz continued. "But so what?" The congratulations coming Tom's way evaporated. "He did his job. That's what we all have to do. The three things. You beat your opposition, your mate beats their opposition, and the team beats the opposition! It's that simple. Now play straight, don't muck around with it, and let's get out there and do it! What's it worth? What's it worth?" He was shouting again, and this time, the boys didn't join in; they just looked at each other, nodding.

They stood up and began to mill around the rooms, slapping each other on the back and muttering clichéd compliments. Albert walked over to Tom, and looked at his lip. "Oooh, brudda. That's going to hurt. You planning on kissing anyone tonight?"

"What? Of course not."

"Good thing. Your lip is so big she'd have to be in another postcode if something was up."

"Albert, shut up, will you? I'm okay. What's up with you?"

"Whaddaya mean?"

"I mean the game. The way you're playing. You're all over the place. You're better than the guy you're on and he's breaking even with you, but every once in a while you torch him. That last handball was amazing, but it's the only Albert thing you've done all day. What are you doing?"

"Nothing, brudda. Just nothing. I'm all good. Remember what I said? It's all about the second half."

"Right. I hope so. After what happened, I just want to smash these guys."

Albert laughed. "Right on, brudda. You got hit so now you want to win? What about before that?"

"Yeah, well, I mean …"

"S'okay, brudda. I know what you meant. Let's do what we need to." Albert slapped him on his sore arm then moved off. Tom followed his movements. The other Aboriginal boys were waiting for Albert, and he moved to them, smiling, and speaking in low tones. Tom heard him say, "We've got this," and then saw him head off to the toilet.

Tom turned his attention to his arm, and George strolled over. "Let me do that for you properly, okay?" As he unrolled a bandage, he spoke in a low tone to Tom. "Don't try and get even. You're not that kid."

"I know," Tom replied. "I want to do something though."

"Of course you do. Just threaten him. Don't do anything, but make him think we're going to purposefully hurt them. Every player. It'll rattle around his head and he won't be able to think of much else. He knows what happened was wrong. We all do. There you go." The bandage was securely taped now, while still giving Tom full movement of his arm.

"How do you know it'll work?"

"Worked on me once. I got told once I'd get knocked out and spent the whole game wondering when I would. Hardly touched the ball out of fear. Never forgotten it."

"Right. Thanks, George."

The old man looked at him and put an enormous hand around

his neck. "Don't thank me, just go and win the bloody game."

The siren rang to let the teams know they needed to get back on the field, and they headed out.

The noise of the crowd had lost a bit of the intensity, but there was still obvious support for them, and for once, Tom looked for his mother but couldn't see her—instead, his eyes fell on Manny, and for a split second he couldn't place her. When he realised who it was he tried to smile, which just hurt his lip. He put his hand to it, and caught her eye—she started laughing too, and yelled, "It's so stupid!" He raised a thumb to acknowledge her, and she waved back. He went past her and onto the field, and the players went to their positions.

Tom again headed to the centre of the ground and looked for Thompson. He too was making his way, and when he saw Tom, his eyes widened. Tom ran towards him and bumped him, hard. "Surprised to see me?" he snarled. "I'm so happy to be back. You don't need to worry about me telling you about the book anymore. We had a raffle at half time."

"A what? Why?" Thompson looked at Tom, not believing what he was hearing.

"Yeah, a raffle. Which one of us would smash you and your gutless prick of a mate when you're at the bottom of a pack. It was number 6, wasn't it? Has he got a name or shall we just call him the Dead Zone? The guy that won the raffle was pretty excited, and he's a nutcase with no remorse and a violent family background. Don't expect that nose of yours to be where it is by the end of the game, either. You ever had a broken nose? They really fucking hurt." Tom bumped him again, hard. "You ready?"

Thompson was silent, trying not to believe what he was hearing. Albert had been standing nearby, and laughed when he heard the exchange. "Oh, man. This is going to be great."

The early minutes of the quarter saw Duneldin quickly extend their lead. They won three centre clearances in a row, one thanks to Tom, and kicked two quick goals. Before anyone knew it, the lead was out to 20 points. Fitz continually yelled at them not to go easy, and after each goal, Mitch, who so far had played well but not done anything to stand out, reminded them it was only the third quarter and that anything could happen. Masterton hadn't gone away, it was just that the gears had clicked for Duneldin. Targets were being hit, tackles were sticking, and the ball bounced their way when they needed it to.

Then the game turned. With the ball in the centre of the ground after a goal, a pack had formed, and a series of ball-ups took place. Albert was wildly slung out of a pack and was paid an obvious free kick for either holding the man or a dangerous tackle. Instead of returning the ball directly to him, a Masterton player threw it away in disgust, giving the umpire no choice but to award a 50 metre penalty. The Duneldin crowd erupted, as this placed Albert easily within his distance, giving him a chance to extend the team's lead to over four goals, the biggest lead of the game.

Albert slowly walked to where the umpire indicated he should kick from, and as he did, most of his teammates started to make their way back to their starting positions, such was the confidence that Albert would kick what for him would be a simple shot from 30 metres out, right in front. As he lined up for goal, Albert looked at Benny and smiled, then looked at his target. He walked in, head down. Instead of kicking smoothly, he took three more steps than he should have, and kicked directly into the man on the mark, the ball ricocheting off his hands and landing just behind him. Before anyone knew what had really happened the ball was whisked to the other end of the ground, and Masterton's full forward was lining up from 20 metres out. He kicked truly, the score was back to 14 points the difference, and Tom and his teammates were in shock.

As they came back to the centre, Tom looked for Albert. When he found him, he asked, "You okay? I thought this was your half."

Albert lifted his head and his eyes bored into Tom's. "It is, brudda. It is. I'm okay, nothing to worry about. Everyone has a miss."

"Not you."

By the time the third quarter had ended, the game's momentum had switched completely. Masterton had scored the last two goals, and Duneldin only led by three points. The boys were quarrelling with each other and pointing fingers as they came to the huddle, demanding of each other what was going on and why mistakes were being made. The bickering only died down when they got to the huddle and all reached for the pre-cut oranges, and started shoving them into their mouths while trying to drink at the same time.

Tom had noticed something that made his eyes go wide—most of the crucial mistakes were being made by the Aboriginal players. Normally the fastest, surest and most creative, they were playing in a way that made them seem second rate. They were being outrun, out bustled and were making basic skill errors, but still doing enough at times to avoid close scrutiny. It was almost as though they were taking it in turns to make mistakes, with Albert at the centre of most of what was going wrong.

Tom didn't want to say anything to anyone else because he wasn't sure but it was becoming clear that as a group, they were purposefully off their game, and not doing anything about trying to fix it. They had again gathered at the back of the huddle and were slapping each other's hands and muttering to each other, and once Tom even saw Benny smile. Tom's stomach had clenched up at the sight of it, realising that whatever the Aboriginal boys were focusing on this Saturday morning, it wasn't winning a flag for the town they lived in.

Fitz had run out of ideas and things to say. He seemed flustered and unsure, and when he tried to repeat his mantra of the day it sounded shallow. He implored the boys to finish out the game and play to their ability, but their collective heads were down and there was little enthusiasm. He quickly went through some small changes to positioning, and before the umpire had blown his whistle to get the teams to come back onto the ground, he had finished his address.

The boys broke, and had started walking back to their positions, only to hear a roar come from their opponents' huddle. The Masterton players broke and ran quickly to their positions, with the midfielders getting to their spots before Tom and his teammates had arrived. Thompson trotted over to Tom and laughed at him. "Mate, I've got a good story for you. It's about the team that won every game in the year then choked in the Grand Final. Have you read it?" Tom looked at his feet, then laughed. "No, it sounds like a piece of shit. Tell me how it ends after the game when you're crying into your mum's hankie and your nose is spread across our goal square."

Time in the last quarter ceased to move logically. In Tom's mind the clock slowed, making its way through mud, and then for some reason raced, skating uncontrollably across ice.

The scoreboard attendant was hardly bothered, as the game

descended from an open-flowing game to a grind, with stoppage after stoppage. When a player did break and had a chance at a free possession often the ball was just moved to another cluster of players, whose desperation meant that another quagmire formed. Tom kept looking for Albert to do something, but he was hardly seen—he stood on the outside of the packs hoping to get a quick handball, but it never came. After 10 minutes Tom had more of the ball than him—two quick kicks out of packs that hit targets, four handballs in traffic and a superb tackle that had seen him awarded a free kick. Tom felt that his influence on the game was growing but he didn't know what to do with it, and at the 15 minute mark of the quarter, when the scores were tied thanks to three rushed behinds to Masterton, he found himself on the half back flank, still shadowing his opponent. "What are we doing here?" he had asked Thompson. "Are they worried you might actually touch the ball or something, or are you scared of getting hit?"

The reason became quickly obvious. They hoped to go through Thompson as a way to goal, meaning Tom's entire focus became standing next to him and anticipating when the ball would come. He remembered to stay on his left, which kept working. Tom could read where he would run and the way he would lead, which meant he could stop any real attack on the ball, and that if Thompson did get the ball, he would be ready to tackle, or bump, or whatever it took. A couple of times when the ball was free enough they did have to compete—all Tom needed to do was bring it to ground and jump on the ball to let a pack form, which he did without giving a free kick away.

Then with the score still level in the dying moments, somehow the game opened up—a handball and two quick kicks got the ball into the Duneldin forward line, but the rushed shot on goal was marked by a lone Masterton player standing in the goal square. There was no-one near him, and he played on immediately, running to the grandstand side of the ground. The next play was a coach's worst nightmare—a long ball from defence that clears a pack; the opponent runs onto it and kicks long. This was the play for Masterton, and before anyone could process it, the ball was headed to a two on two on centre wing.

Now the game was there to be won. The ball fell loose of the contest and a Masterton player, out of desperation and pressure, just hacked at the ball out of the air, kicking it without taking possession, sending it forward. Tom was standing in between two opponents on the half back flank, just inside the 50, this time watching the ball, not minding his man. His immediate reaction to the kick was that hacks like that don't go too far, but this time the connection was sweet. The sound was a pure meeting of boot on leather, and the ball sailed in a perfect arc along the line of the square into the Masterton forward line.

Tom knew that it was his time. As the ball held in the air, he saw an unmarked Masterton player under the ball, and he knew that if he took it, he would turn and kick the ball deep to the goal square. Tom bolted towards the contest, hoping to stop the mark from taking place. As he got closer, he knew that the Masterton player had misjudged the flight, and that he was standing underneath where it would drop. Tom put two huge steps in, and leapt on the player's back, aiming the point of his knee gleefully into the centre of the number 6 he saw there. He struck hard, and as he had always been taught, he used the force of his leap to raise himself further in the air, getting his other knee high enough to set it on his opponent's ear. Instead of trying to mark it, he instinctively punched the ball as hard as he could with both fists, directing it to the centre of the square, where an unmarked Bomber stood, watching the play.

It was Albert. Tom's punch could not have been more perfectly timed or aimed, and it went straight to him. Without thinking or needing to process what had happened, Albert took the ball, and wheeled on to his right foot and took three big steps, launching it quickly into the forward line. The ball went over outstretched hands and fell to the ground. Mitch ran onto it, scooped it up without missing a step, and slammed it goalward. It tumbled towards the goal square, a perfect flat punt that landed and bounced high, holding in the air as if taking a breath, before doing what seemed like an impossible turn, and thumping into the padding at the bottom of the goal post.

With that, Duneldin led by a point. Fitz tried to scream instructions to the boys to get on a player, but his voice was drowned out by all the other noise that surrounded the ground. The Masterton player took the obvious choice and kicked a wobbly torpedo up the centre of the ground, hoping to get to the other end of the ground as soon as possible, but he over-kicked it, and it only travelled 20 metres over the mark. Five players jumped onto the ball to try to win it, and another six surrounded them, and just as the umpire blew his whistle to call for a ball-up, the siren went.

Duneldin had won by the smallest margin, and bedlam ensued.

CHAPTER 10

SATURDAY 7.30 p.m.

By the time Tom, and what appeared to be the whole town, had made their way back to the function room next to the grandstand at Anzac Park, his mind had started to clear. His head was still aching from what was now being described by everyone at the club as "the dog act", but he was now able to process certain things he remembered from the game.

Of course the spoil he had put on was one obvious thing, but beyond that, he thought about the Aboriginal players, and what they had done, or worse, what they hadn't. Albert's plan was now obvious, and had almost come off. If it hadn't been for the luck that always played a part in any game, and for the role that the other team always played in a contest, then what Albert had wanted would now be happening. All the cars would have been driving back to Duneldin with heads bowed and people wondering what happened, instead of a convoy of red and black scarves hanging out of windows, headlights flashing and an incessant beeping of horns.

Tom had begged his mother to go home so he could change, but she insisted that they were all under strict instructions to be at the club by 6.30 p.m. for a short presentation ceremony and a barbeque that Frank Collins had announced for all players and family members to attend as a way of celebrating not just the win, but the whole season—the first time a Duneldin team had gone through a year undefeated in the club's history. So instead of going home and changing his clothes, Tom walked into the club still wearing his team guernsey and club tracksuit pants, with sneakers and no socks to round out his outfit.

Tom swung open the door of the large room where the presentation was to be held and was greeted with a roar. He looked around to see who else had just entered, before realising sheepishly that it was for him. He looked down at the carpet for a second, unsure of how he was to react, then when the sound didn't die down, he raised his head with a reserved grin, and waved. He walked into the room to handshakes and backslaps, people praising him for both his skill and courage, which he tried to bat away, telling everyone it was a team game and that he hadn't really done more than anyone else. This was scoffed at, and when his exploits were being described in the same breath as Hercules, Leigh Matthews and Batman, he knew it was time to get away as soon as possible.

Luckily one person who approached him was Manny, who slipped her arm through his, and, as she always did, whispered, "Tom Wallace, you're still my hero." He took the opportunity to hang on to her arm, and guide her through the glass doors that led to the deck that overlooked the oval as a way of escaping what had already begun to weigh down on him.

When they got to the edge of the deck and were both leaning on the balcony, he let her go, and she turned to face him. She lowered her head and looked up at him, her eyes larger than he had ever seen them. "Why, Tom, did you bring me out here so you could finally seduce me and make all the people who are desperate for us to get together happy?"

"Manny, no-one's that desperate, and we both know that if I was going to seduce you—which I'm not—the last place I would do it is the deck of the footy club in front of a hundred or so people. No, I just wanted to talk to someone who doesn't care about footy. I can't take all that self-congratulation." His eyebrows raised and he looked at her. "Hang on, what are you doing here anyway?"

"Ha! I thought you'd ask. Dad was invited as someone who sponsors the club. He thought I'd want to come and see everyone instead of sitting at home and watching another rented video, so here I am."

"Right. Staying long?"

"No, probably get a sponsor-provided sausage and have a sponsor-provided ice cream then head home. What about you?"

"Same. Even though I should be rapt I can't wait to go home. I can't work out how I feel. I mean, I'm glad we won and it's amazing to see how crazy the town is, but it kind of feels hollow."

"Hollow? How? You won what Dad is describing as a classic, and you were one of the best on the field, apparently. What else do you want?"

"Didn't you see?"

"See what?"

"Albert and the other boys. What they did."

"No. What'd they do?"

Tom looked out to the oval, unsure if he should air his theory. He hadn't told anyone, even his mum in the car on the way home, and if he talked about it now then he'd talk about it again, and eventually someone would find out and take it back to the club, regardless of how much he trusted Manny.

"Oh, don't worry. It's just me being paranoid. I just thought I noticed …" He paused and looked down before continuing. "I thought I noticed them not caring as much. It's nothing."

"Okay. God, you can be so weird. Not caring? If they didn't care, they wouldn't have tried at all, right? And Albert was the one who kicked it in the last bit, right? He must have cared." She grabbed his arm and shook it lightly. "Do you ever get the feeling you overthink stuff? You spend way too much time in that head of yours."

"Yeah, I know. I can't help it." He looked at her and registered her concern. He put his arm around her neck and said, "It's what happens when you're a genius and are surrounded by halfwits." She laughed, and started to respond, when the door to the club opened, and Manny's dad stuck his head out. "Are you two ready to come back in? The presentation is starting."

The formal part of the night was a lively affair—there were a series of speeches, starting with Frank Collins, followed by Fitz, who started crying two sentences in and had to cut his time short because he couldn't stop sobbing, then Mitch. The captain's speech was the one Tom did the most to tune out of—he didn't want to hear a 17-year-old boy who couldn't string an eloquent thought together at the best of times make a speech in public, and he knew that it would be a rip-off of every Premiership captain's speech the kid had ever heard. It was.

Tom was then blindsided by a presentation of a series of awards for the day—the coach and captain were presented with specially struck medals, and then Frank Collins stood at the podium, announcing a new medal, the Barry Green medal for the best player in a Grand Final, named for the last captain of a Senior Premiership side at the club. When Frank called out "Tom Wallace" as the winner, it took half a second for it to register. He stood dumbstruck by the announcement—he had never won anything in his life footy-related—and it took the gentle nudging of a couple of people to get his feet moving towards the stage. He took the three steps up to the platform slowly, then had the medal placed grandly around his neck. He started to make his way back down the steps, when the president grabbed him by the arm and said, "Maybe you should say a few words, son."

He turned back to the microphone, looked down at the blank podium in front of him, then looked up, noticing just how full the room was for the first time. He gently touched his lip, noticing the ache that was still there, and started speaking. "Um, I don't really want to say anything. Premierships are won by teams, not individuals. It's great to get this medal, and thanks to Barry Green, wherever he is. Thanks to the club, thanks to Fitz for his faith, thanks to my mum for the support and clean socks.'" The crowd laughed at this, and his mum waved. "And thanks to Albert Edwards for, well, for everything else."

The crowd looked around for Albert and couldn't see him anywhere. "Well, everything except being here to listen to my speech." Again the crowd laughed, but there was obvious disdain for Albert's absence. "Thanks again, everyone, and have a good night." He walked off stage to more applause, and went through the crowd to his mother. She was standing near the bar in a conversation with a man he didn't know, obviously enjoying herself. "Hey, Mum, have you seen Albert?"

"Hi, Mum, how are you?" she responded.

"Oh, yeah. Sorry. Hi, Mum, how are you?"

"Great." She reached out and hugged him, then leant back. She tugged at the medal around his neck. "Congratulations. Did you know you were getting it?"

"What, this? No. No idea. Didn't even deserve it. Surely there were others better." He looked over her shoulder around the room. "Have you seen Albert? Is he even here?"

"Yes, I saw him earlier, but I think he walked out the door when the speeches started. Can't blame him really. Except for yours they were awful."

"Thanks, Mum. I'm going to try and find him."

"Hang on, I want you to meet someone. Tom, this is Allan Craig. He owns the hardware stores here and in Horminton."

"Oh, right. Hi, Mr Craig. How are you? Look, Mum …"

"Tom, Mr Craig said he enjoyed my article on Albert and Benny and the other Aboriginal boys."

Tom stopped, and looked at his mother, and then across to Mr Craig. "Really? All of it?"

"Yes," he said, smiling. "All of it. I liked it so much that I'm going to spend more on advertising in the paper."

"Wow. That's great. Congrats, Mum."

Jenny smiled, and then tilted her head down. "Not everyone feels the same way apparently."

"What do you mean?"

"There might be a bit less advertising from some areas of town who didn't appreciate the article. Particularly the end. I'm not sure. But Allan—I mean, Mr Craig—tells me not to worry, and that he'll cover whatever is lost."

Tom looked at Allan Craig, a tall man with kind eyes and a big smile. "It's probably time we did something, right? We can't have everyone in the town ignoring …" He stopped, and looked around. "Well, just straight out ignoring, can we?"

"I guess not." Tom looked at his mother and her raised eyebrow.

"Lots of ignoring though, Mr Craig."

"Yep."

Tom looked at them, and then around the club. "Mum, I've got to find him. Albert, I mean. Have you seen him?"

"No, sorry, love. Say hi to him for me when you find him though."

Tom walked outside into the freshness of the evening and looked around. He had no idea where to find Albert or what he would say to him, but he knew he couldn't leave what he knew unsaid. He started walking around the oval towards the entrance gates, when he heard a voice call to him from the grandstand. "Well, brudda. Best on ground, eh?" Tom looked up and saw a lone figure sitting in the stand, feet up on the chair in front. Even though the light had faded, it was obvious who it was.

He climbed the stairs and sat down. Albert turned, sticking out his hand, and without thinking, Tom took it. Albert shook vigorously, a serious look appearing across his face. "Congratulations! Best on ground in a winning Grand Final! In this town, that usually means you'll never have to buy a drink again. Shame you're still underage, but stay here long enough and it'll pay off."

Tom wasn't interested in entertaining Albert's whimsy and forced his hand out of the embrace. "You tried to lose, didn't you." It was a statement rather than a question.

Albert took his feet off the seat in front of him, and finally let Tom's hand go. He slapped a fist into an open palm, and smiled. "You saw it. You're smart. You knew what we were doing. When did you work it out?"

"I'm not that smart. Not really. Not til the third quarter when you missed that goal on purpose." Tom had turned away from Albert, and both boys were now looking out towards the oval.

"Ha! How do you know I did it on purpose?"

"It was a shit kick, and you're never a shit kick. You guys tried to throw it, didn't you?"

"What if we did? So what? Thanks to you, the town's over the moon, and no-one will ever care about how bad we played."

"Don't you?"

"No. We played badly because I wanted us to."

"Why? Why do it?" Tom turned to look at Albert, but his gaze was ignored.

"Why do you think? Do you think they deserve it? Do you think they should get to celebrate?"

"But you'd get to celebrate too. Like Fitz said, we might not get another chance."

"Fitz? That muppet? Spare me." Albert sat forward, his elbows on his knees. "What am I celebrating? The way we get clapped on the back and told how good we are now, then on Monday people cross the street to avoid walking past us? Me or the other boys never getting to be captain? Or that my little brother will have to deal with this too when he wants to play? The celebration's only going to last a few days, but the shit will be never-ending."

"So that …" Tom stopped himself, and looked down.

"Yes, brudda, that's what this is about. It's all it was ever about. I wanted them all to hurt, just for a week or so, so they had an idea about how it felt. But now they won't, so it's all a waste. You and your spoil."

"It was your kick that kept it going!"

"I know! What a dickhead. Couldn't help myself! The rest of the lads are filthy on me," Albert smiled ruefully.

"So what happens now?"

Albert finally looked at Tom. "I'm leaving."

"What?"

"Yep, I'm leaving. As soon as I can. I'm going to a boarding school in Ballarat. I got a phone call from the guys setting up the TAC Cup team there, and they want me to play for them. They've got a connection at a school where I'll get to play as well. I start next term. There's more of a chance for me to get noticed by scouts in Ballarat and then get picked up by an AFL team. That's what I want, almost as much as I want to get out of this shithole."

"But will you come back to play on the weekends like those other kids?"

"Hope not. Hopefully I'll never see the inside of this joint again." His eyes roamed over the grandstand and the scoreboard, then back to Tom.

"Right. When did this all happen?"

"It's been on the boil for a while now. Got the letter from the new club about a month ago, and they linked me up with this school. They talked about me starting next year, but I didn't want to wait. I thought today would be my parting gift, but then you got in the way, you prick." Albert laughed. "Nice medal."

"Thanks, it's meant to be our very own Norm Smith. I don't deserve it though."

"You do, actually. People will only remember a couple of things from this game. You getting smashed and then getting up again and turning the last play will be one of them."

"Do you want it? It should be yours."

"Nup. I didn't want to play well, and I didn't. As much as it shits me to say it"—and again his infectious smile appeared—"you were the better player on the day."

The two boys sat in silence. Finally Tom said, "So will we all get a chance to say goodbye?"

"Mate, it's not like I'm going to the moon. We've still got two weeks of school left and then the holidays. It's a pretty hard town to hide in."

"Right. Of course."

"But right now, I'm goin'. This will go for a while, and I don't want to get into any conversations with anyone I don't respect. I told Mum I'd be home by 8, and it's about that now." He paused. "You gonna tell anyone?"

Tom looked down at his exposed ankles, and the worn concrete below them. "I haven't thought about it. I think I'm the only one who knows. I know why you did it, but I still think it's a shit thing to do. I dunno."

"Well, if you decide to, keep the others out of it. It was my idea, and I'll take it."

"Sure."

Albert was standing now and put his hand out to Tom. Tom looked up at him and took it. "Thanks, brudda. It's been quite the week. See you Monday." Albert turned quickly, and before Tom could reply was down the stairs and walking away.

Tom stood up and watched Albert make his way towards the gate. When he reached the exit, Tom wondered if he would stop and look back, but he didn't. He strode through the exit and halfway across the street. He then turned, and walked purposefully in the middle of the road, heading towards his house.

Tom watched him for as long as he could and, once there was no figure to see, he stood up, heading back into the celebration. As he reached the bottom of the staircase he walked past an old metal garbage bin, where he suddenly stopped. Without really thinking he took the medal from around his neck and dropped it in the bin, and as he heard it clunk in the bottom, he changed his path, making his way home.

ACKNOWLEDGEMENTS

Thanks to the many people who were involved in the backgrounding, proofing and critiquing of this book, including everyone at Fair Play Publishing, Emeritus Professor John Maynard, Amy Edwards, Joe Andrews, Derek Fisher, Jennifer Bourke, Laura Hartmann, Jacinta Francis, Erin McFadyen and Brett Thomas, who knows what he can do.

Finally, it's for Emma, Ed and Anika, who make it worthwhile.

More really
good fiction from
Popcorn Press

Introducing Jarrod Black

Jarrod Black - Hospital Pass

Jarrod Black - Guilty Party

Anna Black - This Girl Can Play

COMING SOON

GAME

Jarrod Black - Chasing Pack

The Gaffer

The Sleeping Giant